QUEENS OF CYBERSPACE

SUZANNE'S DREAM

Clancy Teitelbaum

EPIC
Press

Suzanne's Dream
Queens of Cyberspace: Book #6

Written by Clancy Teitelbaum

Copyright © 2016 by Abdo Consulting Group, Inc.

Published by EPIC Press™
PO Box 398166
Minneapolis, MN 55439

Cover design by Laura Mitchell
Images for cover art obtained from iStockPhoto.com
Edited by Jennifer Skogen

LIBRARY OF CONGRESS CATALOGING-IN-PUBLICATION DATA

Teitelbaum, Clancy.
Suzanne's dream / Clancy Teitelbaum.
p. cm. — (Queens of cyberspace; #6)
Summary: Although it's only been two days in the real world, Brit, Mikayla, and
Suzanne have lived for months in Io. Now, with NPCs turning into monsters and
their allies scarce, the virtual world has never been more dangerous. Their end game
is finally clear: they must return to Zenith City, where their quest started.
ISBN 978-1-68076-202-0 (hardcover)
1. Friendship—Fiction. 2. Computer games—Fiction. 3. Internet—Fiction.
4. Virtual reality—Fiction. 5. Cyberspace—Fiction. 6. Video games—Fiction.
7. Young adult fiction. I. Title.
[Fic]—dc23
2015949428

EPIC
Press

EPICPRESS.COM

For J

Chapter 1

Mikayla Watkins never forgot the first time she saw Suzanne Thurston cry.

Their school, Perry Hall High, was shaped like a horseshoe. The main building had a squashed look to it, like something had stomped on the roof a few dozen times. The north end of the horseshoe was filled with administrative offices. The gymnasium was all the way around the shoe at the southern tip. The main doors for the school opened up to the middle of the curve, so before students were even inside the building they were surrounded by it.

Down by those main doors—well outside the school but still within the reach of the horseshoe's arms—was the dreaded curb. The curb for kids whose parents had to come and get them. Past the curb were bus lines. Riding the bus stank, sometimes literally, but at least the whole school didn't watch you hop into your mom's mini-van if you were a bus kid.

Way, way past the curb was the student parking lot. Most students' careers at Perry Hall High were four-year-long campaigns to nab a parking spot. Mikayla made it there at the beginning of junior year, which was basically unheard of.

There were two ways to get into the student parking lot. Most lot kids came through the main doors, sashaying past curb kids and bus kids en route to the promised land. Seeing those less fortunate reminded the privileged kids to be grateful for what they had, namely, cars and parking spots.

But if you were an athlete, you came right up the south basement steps, direct from the locker room to the south end of the horseshoe. Even if you weren't an athlete with a spot—and freshman year Mikayla had neither car nor parking spot—most teams had enough passes to make a carpool system work.

Most lot kids looked down on the bus and the curb, but athletes didn't even think about them. Not only did they circumvent the dreaded curb and the bus lot, but practices ran so late that by the time they emerged most bus and curb kids were long gone.

Which was why Mikayla was so surprised to see Suzanne sitting curbside at around seven p.m. on a brisk February evening.

Mikayla burst through the basement doors, braced against the cold. She liked to go outside while she was still amped up from practice. The cold air clashed against her sweaty skin. It made her feel awake, ready to go.

She saw the hooded figure seated in the traditional curbside stance—head down, butt on the curb, feet in the gutter. By now, Mikayla knew Suzanne well enough to recognize her at a distance, but even still, she was taken aback to see Suzanne at school so late. Suzanne, Mikayla knew, was a bus kid through and through.

At this point, Mikayla had hung out with Suzanne once or twice. They weren't best friends. Mikayla wasn't sure how good of friends they were. Like, were they just going to play video games with Brit every couple weeks, or was Mikayla supposed to go over to Suzanne and ask her what was wrong? Because, even from that distance, even not knowing Suzanne all that well, Mikayla clearly knew something was wrong.

Mikayla sighed. "Can you wait a minute?" she asked Abby, a senior, who was both the team vice-captain and Mikayla's ride.

Abby took a look at Suzanne buried in her hoodie. She gave Mikayla a look that asked, "Really?" before walking toward the lot.

"I'm leaving in five minutes," Abby called.

Not wanting to miss her ride, Mikayla power-walked around the curb. Either Suzanne couldn't hear her or she was deliberately looking down. But as Mikayla got closer she could see Suzanne's shoulders shuddering. She could see Suzanne had her sleeves over her hands and that she was furiously rubbing at her face.

Mikayla could see Suzanne had been crying.

Despite her efforts to hide her tears, Suzanne's cheeks were red and puffy and her eyes were shining. At some point that day, Suzanne had put her hair in a ponytail, but by the time she was curbside there had been a mutiny, and most of her hair had escaped its tie.

"Are you okay?" Mikayla asked.

Suzanne looked up and her glasses slid down from her forehead to her face. Mikayla was decked out in her post-practice gear: Perry Hall High athletic sweats, a pullover that was essentially a letterman jacket, and hair wrapped up in braids so elaborate that not a single strand could fall out of place. This was before Mikayla cut her hair short.

"Hi," Suzanne said in a thick voice.

Mikayla tried not to frown. "Hi. Are you okay?"

Suzanne looked down at her feet. Mikayla looked down, too. Suzanne's jeans ran out an inch above the ankle, revealing clumsy white cotton socks flecked with gravel and dirt. They were the lamest socks Mikayla had ever seen, and she had a closet full of knee-highs in the colors of home and away games for cheering in colder weather. Suzanne's jeans were cinched at the waist with an overworked belt, designed for someone with a wider frame than their current owner.

"Yeah," Suzanne said. "Maybe. I don't know."

She laughed, which sounded a little bit like a croak.

"Don't I look alright?" she asked.

"Not really," Mikayla replied. And then, she did something semi-unthinkable, at least for an athlete—a parking-lot kid—who'd grown up in Perry Hall High feeder schools and therefore knew the legend of the parking lot and the horror stories of the curb.

Mikayla sat down on the curb next to Suzanne. She felt the cold concrete through her sweats and bits of gravel poked her butt.

Suzanne might not have understood the true magnitude of the gesture. It was, after all, her first year not homeschooled. That didn't matter to Mikayla very much. She fired off a series of questions: "Are you sick?

Is your dad coming? Do you need a ride? Should I get a teacher? Are you gonna throw up? Do you want to talk about it?" What Mikayla was really saying was that she was not just going to go away until Suzanne was really, really okay.

The answer to all of these questions, the last one especially, appeared to be no. Suzanne sat tight-lipped until a sob broke out and the tears turned back on.

Mikayla had seen crying before. She saw girls cry in the locker room all throughout middle school. Mikayla cried herself from time to time—not that she was ashamed of it, but she believed that when the tears were necessary she had a propensity for handling them well. But Suzanne was beginning to full-on wail, hiccuping from tears. Her nose got all snotty.

Mikayla realized Suzanne was quickly slipping beyond her capacity for damage control.

Clumsily, Mikayla thumped Suzanne on the back. Suzanne snapped upright and stared at Mikayla all befuddled.

"Why did you do that?"

"I'm sorry," Mikayla said, involuntarily scooting away from the snotted nose. "I just . . . It's what people do in movies."

Suzanne gave another croaky laugh. Mikayla dug into her gym bag and found a pack of tissues. "Here," she said, tearing a tissue from the pack. "Trust me, you need it."

Suzanne's thank you was muffled by the tissue. She wiped her nose, rubbed her eyes with her sleeves, and took a few full-lung breaths.

"Okay," she said. "Okay, I'm really fine now." She stood up and brushed the dirt off her jeans.

Again, Mikayla was tempted to let Suzanne go. She seemed to be at least operational. If Mikayla started running right now she might make it to the parking lot before Abby left.

"No," Mikayla said. "You aren't okay."

More fake laughing from Suzanne. "It's really nice that you're concerned," she said. She shouldered her backpack and walked around the curb, toward the top of the shoe, and ultimately to Baron Avenue where the city bus stopped. From the student lot, Mikayla heard the honking of a horn and the echo of her name.

Springing up, she began to walk after Suzanne. As Mikayla got closer, Suzanne began to speed up. Her shoulders were shaking and her head was bent forward again. Despite how determined Suzanne was, Mikayla was the athlete. They were neck and neck in no time flat, and this time when Mikayla grabbed at Suzanne's hoodie, Suzanne stopped and spun and shoved Mikayla and said, "What the fuck is your problem?"

"What the fuck is yours?" Mikayla roared back.

"Seriously," Mikayla said, in a quieter, more reasonable voice. "Seriously, Suzanne, what's going on?"

"It's my mom," Suzanne said. She sagged, like she was a puppet and someone had cut her strings. "It's the anniversary or whatever."

Mikayla knew not to ask, *Anniversary of what?* Brit had told her that Suzanne's mom died a year before, which was why Suzanne wasn't homeschooled anymore.

"My dad was supposed to come get me after school,"

Suzanne said. "He was supposed to take me to the cemetery so we . . . so we could . . . " She covered her face with her hands and inhaled deeply.

"So we could visit her. And I think he forgot. I've been waiting since school ended."

That was the first time Mikayla saw Suzanne. Not the geeky Suzanne, the fantasy of every teacher. This wasn't the student who knew all the answers but wouldn't shout them out unless asked. Nor was this Suzanne with her eyes lit up by a game, shouting about frames of animation or controller sensitivity.

This was the Suzanne whose mother had died— Suzanne beyond tears, Suzanne resigned. All Mikayla could do for her was listen and wait until Suzanne's tears subsided. At seven-thirty, they got on the city bus and rode it to Suzanne's street. Mikayla walked Suzanne to the door of her building.

"Thanks," Suzanne mumbled, "you know, for everything."

"Do you want me to come in?" Mikayla asked.

Suzanne shook her head. "No. I'm okay now."

This time Mikayla believed her. She got back on the bus and rode it home. Her mom chewed her out for being so late, for not calling. *What was Mikayla thinking?* her mom wanted to know.

Mikayla was thinking two things. She was thinking how lucky she was to have her mom lecturing her. But mostly, she was thinking about Suzanne and Suzanne's tears. Mikayla never quite forgot about curbside Suzanne, with the limp eyes and resignation written across her face.

Over the next two years, Mikayla never saw Suzanne like that again.

Even when Brit, Suzanne, and Mikayla found out they were stuck in Io, curbside Suzanne didn't reappear. No, that was gamer Suzanne, scheming their escape. When the girls fought the Lamia, when Suzanne lost to Gemini on The Floating Eye, and even when Libra died, Suzanne was down in the dumps but never subterranean. Things were okay as long as they were together.

And then they were separated, then Suzanne was captured. Mikayla convinced Brit that they should go back to Pyxis for help and leave Suzanne a prisoner in the Fenlands of Altair. Brit tried to steer the conversation away from Suzanne, but Mikayla couldn't stop thinking about her. Whenever Mikayla pictured Suzanne in chains she couldn't. Instead, Mikayla pictured Suzanne as she had been on that curb. It wasn't until Mikayla and Brit found Suzanne, self-liberated in a Pyxian town called Glensia, that Mikayla realized that things had changed.

Suzanne was in Glensia's Oratorium when Mikayla found her. There were Oratoriums in every town in Pyxis—domed buildings filled with statues of deceased NPCs. Unusually, Glensia was littered with statues of NPCs. But these statues, unlike the ones in the Oratorium, were sculpted in terror.

Burgrave and Crux, two old enemies, were waiting for them. Mikayla and Brit were ready for a fight, but

Burgrave lay down his sword and directed the girls to the Oratorium and Suzanne.

For an hour, it was just like their first days in Io, when the three of them could game without worry. As the sun began to set, Mikayla felt her fear settle, the nervous energy which had been building since Suzanne was captured uncoiled into relief. The girls took some time to fill each other in on what they had learned while separated. Mikayla told Suzanne that Leo, the king of Pyxis, was no longer someone they could count as a friend. But three high-ranking Pyxians were half a day's journey away from Glensia. Suzanne explained that the statues around Glensia were Citizens, the class of NPC reserved for non-combat characters. At least Suzanne had good news: she now had the key to the Oracle Chamber, the last thing the girls needed to escape from the game. Mikayla barely had time to register they would soon be free before everything went to hell.

They were so engrossed in each other's company that they missed the changes happening to the statues in Glensia. They grew claws on their hands and fangs in their mouths. The stone skin became coarse and the creatures turned feral. It took Brit, Mikayla, and Suzanne's combined efforts to put the first one of the creatures down.

Burgrave and Crux came running over as the first gargoyle pixelated. And then Gemini, Suzanne's insane doppelgänger, showed up. As the Assassin taunted Mikayla and her friends, the other Citizens in the town transformed and attacked the party. More of the creatures surged into Glensia—the Citizens of the surrounding towns, bent to Gemini's cause. The Assassin went right for Suzanne. With all the gargoyles running around, Mikayla couldn't keep track of Suzanne's fight.

The party managed to regroup in the town square. Suzanne was there, banged up from her fight but glowing with her victory. *We can do this,* Mikayla thought. *We can win.*

Mikayla was staring at the former Citizens, watching as they formed up into a loose phalanx. So Mikayla didn't see the dagger go into Suzanne. But she heard

Suzanne mutter a soft, "Oh," and saw Gemini running away and Gemini's dagger planted in Suzanne's back.

And then Mikayla saw it.

It was that look. That blank, curbside resignation. That acknowledgement that things hurt. Things go wrong. Sometimes you can't apologize for the world and what it does, regardless of whether the world is real or virtual.

Suzanne fell.

Mikayla waited for her to get up. She had seen Suzanne kill monsters. Once, Suzanne jumped off a cliff to save Brit's life. Anything was possible in Io— that was why Suzanne had made this world.

Suzanne had to get up.

She did not. She struggled to her knees. Holding her side, she spoke in a low, surprised voice that cut through the sounds of battle and hit Mikayla in the chest like a punch. "Must be some glitch. I feel totally fine."

Before Mikayla could reply, Suzanne was gone.

Chapter 2

Brit heard Mikayla scream.

Was Io ever real for her until that scream? Even the NPCs, programmed with personalities, fell in that uncanny valley of artificial intelligence—of life that never felt quite right. They were more realistic than any other game character, but the gray icons that twirled over their heads coupled with their other idiosyncrasies of speech and behavior never let Brit forget that all the NPCs in Io had been generated by an algorithm Suzanne wrote. Despite damage and imprisonment and the fact that they couldn't log out, Brit had never stopped believing that none of it, not one part, was truly happening.

She didn't always remember her real, under-five-foot body, but she knew her massive Dragoon frame was borrowed and temporary. So when she took damage, she knew she wasn't really hurt. Even if Mikayla and Suze reacted a little more dramatically, Brit firmly believed they would be okay. She never forgot she was playing a game.

Brit was rushing toward the Citizens, a step behind Crux, when she heard Mikayla scream. She turned around and saw Mikayla had collapsed. She saw a cloud of pixels. She did not see Suzanne. It took Brit another two seconds to figure it out. Then, rage.

A Citizen saw her distracted and leapt at her. They had skin like stone, these gargoyles. No one in the party had been able to cut them. Brit caught the creature at the throat with her free hand. It writhed, trying to slash at her. Brit saw a small flesh-colored circle at the base of its neck. She dropped her halberd and jammed her fingers into the fleshy spot. With a single wrenching motion, she pulled its head from its shoulders.

She dropped the Citizen's body. Certain things did not make sense to her. She picked up her halberd. A Citizen jumped on her back while she was bent over. Brit smashed her fist into its head until the creature was still.

The creatures swarmed Crux. He was even bigger than Brit, but there were so many of them they were able to bring the massive Dragoon to the ground. Burgrave, a Swiftblade like Mikayla, was blocking swiping claws. But that was all he could do. His sword couldn't cut through their skin.

"The back of the neck!" Brit roared. Burgrave sidestepped a slash and hacked at the back of the Citizen's neck. The creature's head came free of its shoulders, pixelating instantly.

Mikayla was still on her knees, covering her face with her hands. Two Citizens were approaching her. Brit tackled the gargoyles and smashed their heads into each other until they cracked into pixels. Her experience points trickled upwards. But something wasn't balancing out.

The Citizen horde closed in on all sides. Brit saw, over their heads, Gemini limping off. Glensia wasn't a large town, and Brit could clearly see its limits. Just beyond Glensia was a tangle of trees, the perfect place for Gemini to retreat—no, run away. *Well, that's just unacceptable*, Brit thought.

"Wait," she whispered.

The others could take care of themselves. Brit waded forward into the battle, battering the Citizens out of the way. If she could just get to Gemini things would balance out. Balance out what, she couldn't say. But as long as she got to the Assassin things would be okay.

Something scratched at her leg, and she looked down to see a Citizen with its claws dug in. She lifted her leg and shook it off like a flea. Then she stomped on its head. Then she stomped on its head again. A clawed hand flopped over, pixelating.

"Wait," Brit said. Who was she speaking to? Gemini couldn't hear her and wouldn't have waited regardless. The Assassin ducked around a corner, vanishing from view. Brit stomped down a Citizen and knocked over what had once been a home and spotted Gemini sprinting past the inn.

"Wait," Brit said again, a little louder. A Citizen stepped in front of her and Brit grabbed it by the shoulders, hurling it into a building. Gemini was further away, nearly at the village fence. The woods loomed beyond the Assassin, promising escape.

"Wait!" And now Brit was shouting, running through the Citizens like they were blades of grass. Claws nicked her health bar down bit by bit but that really didn't matter to her, nothing much mattered to her except the Assassin who was running away. Yet for every Citizen she cut through, six more appeared where it had been.

Where were they all coming from? Brit didn't care to think of an answer. She sent them all to the same place.

Brit heard someone shout her name. It reached her as a faint echo. Her rage was much louder. But now she was mired in Citizens. She glanced back. They were behind her, encircling her. She saw Mikayla standing and fighting alongside Crux and Burgrave. Their eyes met for a second and Brit saw interminable sadness in Mikayla.

She had no idea what Mikayla saw when the Citizens swarmed her. They grabbed every inch that could be grabbed. By sheer numbers, they brought her down to one knee. Claws raked at her face and back and arms. Before gray stony skin blocked out the sky and turned her world into a wave of slate, Brit saw Gemini reach the fence and cross into the woods.

Then the mass of bodies closed and she couldn't see anything. She closed her eyes. She remembered Suzanne's face.

"Wait!" Brit erupted from the Citizens like an expletive. The creatures were thrown off her, but they sprang back up and encircled her again. Brit glanced up at her health bar and saw it was half gone. A different fear clutched at Brit.

"Mikayla!" she roared. "Mikayla!"

Brit heard Mikayla calling her name and saw her. She was backed into a corner. The blade of one of her swords had snapped off at the hilt. Burgrave, disarmed, stood panting with his hands on his knees beside her. Crux was keeping the gargoyles away with wide sweeps of his hammer, but the creatures were poised to rush them at any moment.

Brit turned back. She hated herself for doing it, but she didn't have a choice. Somewhere in the woods Gemini was escaping, and Brit had to let her go.

She lowered her shoulder and charged into the wall of gargoyles. They didn't get out of the way. The creatures were absolutely fearless, slashing at Brit even as she ran them over. By the time she broke through to the rest of her party, her health was down to a third—glaring yellow at the periphery of her vision.

Crux checked his hammer so Brit could slip by. Her whole body shook with exhaustion.

"Are you okay?" Mikayla asked.

Brit didn't answer. She didn't know how to answer.

Some undetectable signal passed between the remaining Citizens. The gargoyles massed in front of the party. Those that had been lunging at Crux backed up into their ranks.

"Burgrave," Crux muttered. He stopped swinging his hammer and held it in front of him, ready to bear the brunt of the gargoyles' assault.

"I see," Burgrave said. "There are too many to stop." As always, the diminutive NPC spoke calmly. Which only furthered Brit's sense of hopelessness.

"Well, fuck it," Mikayla said. Brit looked at her, surprised. "If we're going down, let's take them with us." Mikayla threw her broken sword down and withdrew another from her inventory. Mikayla moved to Crux's side. She looked tiny next to the massive Dragoon, her swords like toothpicks.

Brit couldn't help herself. A crazy smile formed on her lips. She took a heavier halberd from her inventory. If she couldn't hack through the gargoyles she could at least smash them. She stood beside Mikayla, ready to end things one way or the other. Burgrave took out another scimitar and walked to Crux's other side.

Four of them against the horde.

The gargoyles snarled and scraped their claws against each other. Lined up like this, Brit saw there were still dozens of them. She almost laughed.

One at the front threw back its head and howled, charging at the party. An axe came whirling out of nowhere. The projectile slammed into the Citizen's shoulder, spinning it around. Brit turned with the rest of the party and saw Alphonse enter Glensia.

The Adept ran at full speed toward the creatures. He wasn't as big as Brit or Crux, but he also wore almost no armor. Two steps behind him was Lynx, her double-blade naginata spinning in her hands. Mallon brought up the rear, her whip uncoiled, whirling it like a rope-dancer in an Old West show.

Alphonse dropped and slid into the front line of the horde, knocking the creatures' legs out from under them. In a flash Lynx was on them, ramming the blade of her weapon into the back of the creatures' necks.

To Brit's surprise, the naginata didn't bounce off. The creature howled in what must have been pain as its body began to pixelate. The gray creature burst into pixels. None of the other Citizens responded at all, unfazed by their newfound vulnerability. Normal monsters in Io retreated when they were outmatched, but it didn't seem like the Citizens could conceive of defeat and death.

"What are we waiting for?" Brit shouted. She charged forward, Mikayla half a step behind her. Brit trucked into the nearest gargoyle, flipping it over her shoulders. Mikayla stabbed at its neck three times, the third strike piercing through the weak spot, killing the creature instantly.

"Stand together!" Lynx cried. "We end them here!" Bolstered by the Pyxians, the party cut through the horde, cleaving a path toward the edge of Glensia. Brit lost track of how many of the creatures she had killed. She tried not to think of them as Citizens, but traces of their former class remained. The smaller ones must have been children, Brit realized, but she forced herself to focus on the battle. She could deal with guilt later.

The horde was reduced to fifteen. They were moving slowly, as if they had lost the desire to battle.

But the party didn't take any chances. As Crux smashed the last of the creatures down to nothing, Brit charged toward the woods where Gemini had escaped. By the time she reached the trees, Brit realized she had no idea where the Assassin had gone. Whatever trail there might have been was completely obscured by the trampling horde.

No! she thought, and the word escaped as a growl. "No," she growled again.

Brit felt a hand on her shoulder and she whirled around, swinging her halberd. It was Mikayla. Brit checked her blow. The halberd flew out of her hands and buried itself in a tree trunk. The tree pixelated, vanishing.

Like Suzanne.

"Brit." Mikayla's voice was soft. She put a hand on Brit's cheek.

It didn't feel soft to Brit, the hand. It didn't feel like anything but digital weight. Her character registered the contact but what Brit felt was anguish creeping out from her heart, spreading to every inch of her body.

And then Brit felt the pain from every single slash, the full pain of three-quarters of her health bar lost to the Citizens. It was suddenly very real for her, the damage, the danger, all of it.

"Brit," Mikayla said again.

Brit looked down at her best friend in this world or any other. A green diamond twirled over Mikayla's head, marking her as a player character. Brit understood that now she and Mikayla were the only people in all of Io. Everyone else was an NPC.

She wrapped her arms around Mikayla and held her close. "I won't let you go," Brit whispered. Mikayla didn't say anything. She just held on to Brit.

Somewhere back in Glensia, Suzanne had died. Brit knew the exact spot was as unfindable as Gemini. The game mechanics left the ground unblemished by blood or a body. Brit added that to the list of injustices. Brit held Mikayla, and she sobbed dry sobs until she became overwhelmed and could not understand how the minutes were passing with Suzanne dead. Then Brit collapsed.

Chapter 3

An hour later, Brit woke up to the pressure of a palm on her forehead.

"I'm no healer," Mallon was saying. "This was always more your brother's specialty. She'll be fine but that's more to do with her than anything I could do."

"We need her," Lynx replied.

Brit's eyes snapped open. The sun seemed too bright, considering Lynx and Mallon were standing over her. Mallon had her hand on Brit's forehead, but pulled it away.

"How do you feel?" she asked.

Brit glanced up at her health bar—it was now half-full again. Then she remembered.

"Terrible," Brit said.

She was lying on the ground. She rolled over to her hands and knees, bracing herself before standing.

"Where's Mikayla?" she asked.

"In the Inn, with Burgrave," Mallon answered. Brit blinked her eyes a couple of times, trying to adjust to the light. She wasn't adjusting. Somewhat appropriately, Glensia was in ruins. Not a single building still had all its walls. Several had pixelated completely.

"Brit," Lynx said. "I know you must feel terrible right now."

"No. You don't."

"I do," Lynx insisted. "I lost my brother, I lost Alphonse and now Suzanne."

Anger seized Brit. She stepped up to Lynx. She towered over the princess and glared down at her.

"Listen. You don't know. You think . . . " The anger left her as suddenly as it had come, leaving her deflated and wordless. Brit swayed—the breeze would knock her over right now. What could she possibly say to Lynx to make the NPC understand?

"I'm going to go talk to Mikayla," Brit said. Her voice was hoarse. It sounded alien, like someone put the words in her throat.

She brushed past Lynx and half-walked, half-stumbled toward the Tear of the Troll, Glensia's inn. She pushed the door open. The inside was dark, unlit except for what light trickled in through the windows. A memory hit Brit suddenly, the memory of the first inn Brit entered in Io. So much of the Tear of the Troll was the same as the Belching Minotaur: same dusty interior, same crooked bar, same drab fireplace. She had arrived at the Belching Minotaur with Mikayla and Suzanne on their first day in Io proper, their first day out of the tutorial level known as the Meadow of Beginnings.

Brit and Mikayla had followed Suzanne into the inn, even though they weren't hurt, because that's what you did in games. You chatted with innkeepers and spent the night to trigger the next event. Io had been so full of promise then. Hawthorne the innkeeper had charged them all their gold for a night's stay.

Brit was the only one of the three of them against it. Remembering how vehemently she had argued against spending their gold, it made her cringe now. None of that had mattered. All the gold was gone now, along with the banter and bickering between her and her friends. And without that laughter and teasing the inn felt darker, empty despite Burgrave and Mikayla sitting there.

At a table by the bar sat Mikayla and Burgrave. A small stein of what looked like beer was in front of the bald NPC. Burgrave raised his stein to Brit, took a sip, set it down. The click of mug on wood echoed through the room.

Mikayla's hands lay palm up on the table in front of her. They were the sole focus of her attention.

"Can we have a minute?" Brit said to Burgrave.

He didn't argue, merely rose and made for the door. He paused beside Brit. Brit hoped he wasn't going to say anything. She felt like she was going to explode or implode at any minute. Apparently, Burgrave sensed that and left without another word.

Good. Or as good as anything could be.

Brit crossed the room and pulled back a chair. She sat herself down gingerly. Through all of it, Mikayla stared at her palms like they were the most interesting things in the world.

Brit opened her mouth, but what could she say? All words were stupid. She let her mouth shut and in silence watched Mikayla.

"She had the key." Mikayla spoke without inflection, her voice drained of emotion.

"What?"

"Remember? She showed us right before the fight. The key to the Oracle Chamber. We could have gone home. We were going home."

Mikayla looked like she was about to cry. But she couldn't. Crying wasn't programmed into Io's code. Brit's brain stumbled over words, searching for the right ones. But there weren't any right ones.

"Remember—" Mikayla began, but the words caught in her throat and she stopped.

The word *remember* is a tricky thing. When

Mikayla said, "Remember," Brit felt the word like a jolt of electricity. Now Suzanne was to be remembered. Now she was past tense.

Mikayla swallowed and forced out the rest of the sentence. "Remember how happy she was?" Mikayla asked.

Brit felt it hurt and knew Mikayla must be feeling the same emptiness. She reached out and grabbed Mikayla's hand and squeezed it. This time, Brit felt Mikayla's touch. She felt the warmth of another body, even a digital one, and the virtual world seemed a little less desolate.

When Brit spoke it came as a whisper. "We don't know for sure . . ." She couldn't bring herself to finish the sentence. They didn't know for sure what had happened to Suzanne, but her avatar's body was gone.

They let that small hope float in the air. For a few minutes, neither of them were willing to break the silence and burst that hope.

Eventually, Mikayla sighed. "I feel like I'm trespassing," she said. "That's what this feels like."

"*We're* trespassing," Brit corrected her. "And we aren't. This is still Suzanne's world and she invited us here in the first place."

"What are we going to do now?" Mikayla said. "What the fuck are we going to do?"

Mikayla looked at her expectantly, and Brit realized she knew exactly what they had to do.

"I don't know long term. But the first thing we're doing is getting even. We're gonna march up to the Pyxian camp and get the whole fucking Pyxian Army behind us and we're gonna get even."

Mikayla didn't reply. Brit muscled on even though the words were getting caught in her throat.

"We're gonna find Gemini and kill her. And Xenos. And Ramses."

"Ramses is dead," Mikayla interjected. "Suze—she told us that."

"Yeah. Yeah, okay. So we find Gemini, we find Xenos, and we end them."

Brit couldn't read Mikayla's expression.

"That's it?" Mikayla asked.

"That's it," Brit replied. "That's the entire plan."

"How are we getting home?"

"I don't care about that. First things first. We get even."

Even as Brit said the words, she knew they were a lie. No number of NPCs would equal Suzanne. But the math made enough sense for right now.

Mikayla gave her a thin smile. She knew Brit was lying and Brit knew she knew. But Brit also knew Mikayla wasn't going to call her on it. Mikayla was going to let her be brave and blustery. And Brit loved Mikayla for that, for letting her recede into a stereotype.

Brit could play the part. She smashed her fist through the table. The stein fell and cracked, spilling its contents everywhere. Brit rose violently, knocking back her chair. As the split table broke into pixels she stomped on the mug and ground it into dust.

Next up was the chair. Brit whipped it at the wall, smashing the chair into pieces, and tearing the canvas of a painting hanging there. Brit strode across the room and ripped the frame off the wall, breaking it in half over her knee. She tossed both halves into the fire. The game combusted them before the wood hit the flames.

She heard the sound of breaking glass behind her and whirled around to see Mikayla standing on the bar. On the floor were shards of broken mug. In her hand was another. Mikayla kicked out her leg like a pitcher and threw the mug at the ground. The sprinkles of glass dust shot across the floor, skittering into Brit before they pixilated.

Brit turned back toward the fireplace to keep her smile to herself. She gripped both ends of the fireplace mantle and pulled, ripping it out of the wall. She sent the mantle crashing into more of the tables, coming to rest by the opposite wall.

Mikayla had drawn her swords and was dicing up the remaining tables and chairs. Her blades moved so fast that she was already slicing at the next object while the previous one was falling apart. As she relieved the inn of its furnishing, Mikayla's face sank into a mask of concentration. For the moment, at least, she could focus on something else.

Brit left the common room to Mikayla. She went up the stairs and smashed through the door of a bedroom. She shattered the end table, punched out the windows. She took a swing at the bed, but the mattress wouldn't break. Well, whatever. There was still the rest of the inn to take care of.

Running back down the stairs, Brit punched a couple of holes in the wall. Mikayla was finishing off the furniture, so Brit crossed the room toward the bar. She placed both hands under the bar and heaved with all of her strength. The counter didn't budge at first, but slowly, with the sound of snapping foundations, it began to give way. With one final shove Brit ripped it all the way free. Grunting from exertion, she curled the bar. She took two small steps back and three quick ones forward, heaving the bar at the front door.

It smashed through the wall. The magic of Io's physics engine left the other three standing. Once the dust and pixels settled, Brit saw Burgrave standing in front of the Tear of the Troll, his hand poised as if about to knock on the door.

"It is, ah, time we left," Burgrave said. "Our enemies will be sending reinforcements to this location."

Brit felt Mikayla's hand slide into hers. She recoiled reflexively at the contact. Then she grabbed onto Mikayla's hand and didn't let go. Hand in hand, they left the ruins of the bar and Glensia behind them.

Chapter 4

"We should arrive in another day," Lynx said. "Or by sunrise after at the latest."

"And you said you have an army?" Brit asked.

Lynx shook her head. "Not an army. Free Pyxians, who will fight against Xenos until they draw their last breath."

Assuming they haven't already been turned into those creatures, Mikayla thought. But there was no point in voicing what everyone in the party knew, NPC or human. If the graying that turned Glensia's Citizens into monsters hit the Pyxian camp, then the party was walking into a trap.

But again, Mikayla kept her fears to herself.

They were traveling hard north over the Pyxian plains. Mikayla didn't know if it was her imagination or what, but all the color seemed to be leaking out of the world. The first time she was in Pyxis, barely two months ago of in-game time, the savannah was a lush green, like the Meadow of Beginnings. But now it was more like a scrubland, the grass dry and brittle, pixelating as the party brushed through.

The few creatures Mikayla saw fled from the party. A group of kobolds kicked up a cloud of pixels as they turned tail and fled. Brit hurled a hand-axe after them, nailing the slowest right in its scaly back.

"Did I hit it?" Brit asked.

Mikayla peered into the distance, using her class abilities to distinguish the little loot box left in the kobold's wake.

"Yeah," she said. "Good shot."

Brit said nothing. She didn't go to retrieve her hand-axe. Mikayla had the sneaking suspicion Brit was practicing for Gemini. It was a day after the party left Glensia. Without much discussion, she and Brit had stuck with the NPCs. Sure, they were going after Xenos, but they needed an army. Xenos had the Altairi Army on his side, and maybe the Pyxian Army too. Mikayla knew she'd have to take any help she could get, even if it was just a bunch of peace-loving Pyxians.

Not too long after the kobold confrontation, Mallon and Burgrave returned. They had been scouting ahead of the party, leaving Mikayla with Brit, Crux, Lynx, and Alphonse. The Pyxians and the Altairi in the party didn't trust each other at all. Mikayla had hoped that Burgrave's and Crux's fugitive status would help Lynx and the other Pyxians trust them. They were all NPCs after all. But she had underestimated how the war between Pyxis and Altair had absolutely divided the two nations. It didn't help that Burgrave was formerly Ramses's chief advisor.

Having Mallon and Burgrave scout together was the only compromise that worked. Alphonse refused to leave Lynx alone, and Burgrave didn't trust Crux alone with any of the Pyxians. And it wasn't like Mikayla was willing to let Brit out of her sight. She was done with splitting up. So Burgrave and Mallon were the scouts.

"The area ahead appears clear," Burgrave said.

Even though Burgrave was a Swiftblade, the same class as Mikayla, they looked totally different. Burgrave was a foot shorter and completely bald. He wore chainmail armor, concealed beneath a loose Pyxian robe. Burgrave normally wore ruby earrings which dangled on long chains, but since she encountered the NPC in Glensia he hadn't been wearing them.

"We saw no villages and no Citizens, monstrous or otherwise," Burgrave said.

"There's a bit of a valley up ahead, a few trees spread around it. Hard to see in, and the slopes make the way in fairly narrow. Might make a nice place to stop for the night," Mallon suggested. The silver-haired Monk was the oldest NPC in the party. Of all the NPCs in the party, only Mallon had access to healing abilities, but they weren't a specialty of her class. She tucked her long braid over her shoulder. "If we take turns at watch, put sentinels at each end and another by the sleepers, we should be okay."

"What do you think?" Lynx asked Alphonse. The Pyxian princess was tall and athletic. Mikayla could imagine Lynx being a rock star on the cheer squad, if this was the real world. Since Glensia, Lynx hadn't set her naginata down. She was dressed in a plain, tan Pyxian robe despite her nobility.

Alphonse thought for a moment before answering Lynx's question. "The valley seems like our best option. If we do not rest soon we will become sloppy and the enemy will take us."

"Then it is decided," Lynx said. "We head for the valley."

As the sun was setting, the party found the area Mallon had described. Crux, the massive Altairi Dragoon, rolled a boulder into the mouth of the valley. It wouldn't stop those Citizen creatures, Mikayla knew, but it might slow them down.

While the NPCs set up camp, Mikayla and Brit went off to set up their tent.

As they worked, Mikayla watched Brit. Brit had her armor off. At a moment's notice she could reequip all of her gear, popping it back on with a few gestures in her Player Menu. Even so, Mikayla thought Brit was tempting fate not wearing it. But Mikayla didn't want to argue about wearing armor.

Without the bulky plate mail, Brit's size was less cartoonish. She was still nearly seven feet tall, still a pile of long muscles. It was funny, Mikayla thought. She and Brit had only been together—been more than just friends—in Io, where Mikayla came up to Brit's chin. In the real world, things were the other way around. Brit was barely five feet tall.

"What are you looking at?" Brit asked. Mikayla realized she had just been staring at Brit.

"Um, nothing," Mikayla said.

Brit gave her a half-amused smile. "You've been staring at me for like five minutes. What's up, Watkins?"

"I was just thinking," Mikayla said. "You know, about us."

"What about us?" Brit asked. She set the tent down. Her little smile was gone.

"It's just . . . what's going to happen to us when we get home?"

Brit laughed. "Shit, you had me scared for a second. Don't we have other things to worry about?"

Mikayla kicked a rock over with her toes. "I shouldn't have said anything." She picked up the tent and secured the last corner, which turned the item into a fully pitched tent big enough for two. Mikayla lifted the flap and climbed inside.

After a moment, Brit climbed in after her.

"*When* we get out of here," she said, "you'll have to be the big spoon. That's it."

"Assuming that you still want to, you know, be together," Brit added.

"Of course!" Mikayla said. Brit laughed again, and Mikayla laughed, too.

"Good," Brit said. "I don't know if I could take you dumping me the same week Suzanne got killed."

Mikayla cringed. "Too soon. Way too fucking soon.

I mean, we still don't know if she's really, you know, gone."

"Sorry," Brit said. Outside the tent, dusk fell. Mikayla watched the light filtering through the canvas turn a deep red and then vanish into indigo night.

"It doesn't even feel like she's really gone," Mikayla said. "Like when Ramses had her kidnapped, you know how you said she was okay? It felt like we would know if she was really hurt. I don't know why, but that's how it felt."

Brit shrugged. "Maybe because we're all hooked up to the TII. But you're right. Like part of it just feels like when we were bumming around Pyxis without her. But I saw what Gemini did. I saw the pixels . . ." Her voice cracked. "It's my fault, isn't it?"

Brit's face was covered by the shadow of night. "What the hell are you talking about?" Mikayla asked. "You aren't Gemini. How is it your fault?"

"I told her to put permanent death in. If it wasn't for me she'd just re-spawn. We would have never been stuck here." She shook her head. "It's my fault."

Mikayla leaned over and kissed her on the cheek. "Shut up," she said.

Brit refused to look at her. So Mikayla cupped her hands around Brit's chin and turned her head—no mean feat considering the tendons in Brit's neck. Locking eyes, Mikayla spoke slowly and deliberately. "This is not your fault," she said. "And if you blame yourself again, I'm going to have to kick your ass."

Brit smiled and was about to say something back when outside the tent Lynx shouted, "I will not endanger my people!"

"This is no way to protect them!" That was Burgrave, and he was shouting. Mikayla didn't know if she had heard him shout before. She left the tent with Brit behind her and found Lynx and Burgrave staring at each other in the center of camp, the other NPCs gathered around them.

"What's going on?" Mikayla asked.

"This . . . This Altairi," Lynx said, spitting out Burgrave's nationality like it was a dirty word, "will not listen to common sense. I will not allow him to enter the camp with us. He is too much of a danger to the Pyxians!"

"And I say she is blind!" Burgrave yelled. His fists were clenched in anger. "Crux and I were allies of Suzanne. Whatever we have done in the past is in the past. We all face a greater danger now, worse than any petty war between our nations!"

He took a step toward Lynx and Alphonse immediately jumped between them.

"Do not move any closer," the Adept growled. He gripped the handle of his axe like he intended to use it.

"Back down, Alphonse," Brit said. "You don't want to start this fight."

"I will protect the princess," Alphonse replied haughtily.

"Burgrave is not trying to hurt Lynx!" Crux rumbled.

"No one wants to hurt anyone," Mikayla said. She stepped into the middle of the NPCs and raised her hands away from her swords. "We're all on the same side here."

"For now!" Lynx snarled. "There's no guarantee these two won't betray us. I don't know how Suzanne trusted them in the first place, after all they've done!"

Before Mikayla could stop herself her sword was out and at Lynx's throat. Alphonse made to get in the way, but Brit grabbed him and held him back. Lynx's eyes narrowed as she stared down the point of Mikayla's estoc.

"Don't," Mikayla hissed. "Don't say shit about Suzanne."

"Are you insane?" Lynx asked.

"No," Mikayla replied. After a moment she pulled her sword away and shoved it back in its sheath. "Maybe desperate. We're all desperate right now and we need all the help we can get."

Everyone, player and NPC, stared at each other, waiting for someone to move. Mikayla knew that, with them all at such high levels, a fight wouldn't leave many survivors.

Mallon coughed politely. Everyone turned to stare at her.

"Can't say I care for her method of going about it, but it seems like Mikayla's got a point here. Literally, I might add. We need each other now."

Lynx looked like she was about to argue, but she relented. "Very well." Speaking to Burgrave, she added, "I may not trust you, but it is enough that my allies do. For now. Do not give me a reason to doubt their judgment."

And to Mikayla, she added, "If you ever draw steel against me again I will make sure it is the last time."

With that, she turned and stalked toward her tent. Alphonse glared at Mikayla before following his princess.

"My thanks," Burgrave said, bowing to Mikayla and Mallon. "I assure you I am completely on your side."

"Think nothing of it," Mallon replied. "You're the first watch."

Mikayla and Brit went back to their tent. Now, more than before, Mikayla hoped they got to the Pyxian camp soon. Back among her people, maybe Lynx could relax.

Chapter 5

Brit had fond memories of the Pyxian camp from the last time she had passed through. The last time she was with the Pyxians, they had welcomed her and her friends with open arms. Of course, it didn't hurt that they were traveling with Lynx and Leo. This was back before kingship, before Xenos changed Leo, back when he and Lynx were showing Brit and her friends Pyxis for the first time. The Pyxian camp had been an easygoing place, and Brit still remembered the carefree night she spent with friends around a fireplace, drinking Pyxian wine and letting their worries go.

Back then, the Pyxians had been at war with the Altairi. Yet despite the war, the Pyxians were unguarded in their kindness. Now, as the party approached the camp, they were met by a detachment of armed Citizens.

Mikayla cupped her hands over her eyes, scanning the NPCs racing toward them.

"They don't look like they've changed," Mikayla said. Brit and everyone else in the party exhaled. That was one less thing they had to worry about. There were five Citizens in total, all armed with the makeshift weaponry Citizens always fought with. They were fearless, Brit had to admit that much. But she didn't doubt for a moment that anyone in her party could handle all five of them.

When they saw Lynx was traveling with the party, the Citizens were visibly relieved. That only confirmed Brit's suspicions. *This is our army for fighting Xenos?* But Brit had to remind herself that Pyxian Citizens were better than nothing.

The leader of the Citizens appeared to be the most competent of their party. She was taller than the other Citizens and held her makeshift spear with more comfort than the others. She bowed low to Lynx and said, "They will be much relieved by your return, Princess."

Lynx offered a thin smile. "Thank you, Gemma. I have brought powerful fighters with me as well."

Gemma regarded the rest of the party. "I can see that they are of advanced class. They will help us greatly in retaking our kingdom."

"We're glad to be here," Mikayla said. Brit gave her a sidelong look, and Mikayla shrugged.

"Well, we are," she whispered.

"My pardon," Gemma said. "But are you Mikayla of The Floating Eye."

Mikayla nodded. "Lynx said your name is Gemma, right? It's nice to meet you."

Gemma smiled and bowed as she had bowed to Lynx. "That must mean you are Lady Brit."

"Yeah, whatever," Brit said.

"Is Lady Suzanne here? She was also in your party, right?"

Brit's heart skipped a beat. She didn't know how to form the obvious words.

"Lady Suzanne was taken from us," Burgrave intoned. "It happened recently. Brit and Mikayla are still grieving."

A look of horror spread across Gemma's face. "I'm so sorry!" she stammered. "I had no idea! I apologize for my insensitivity."

Brit wasn't about to accept condolences from some random NPC. "Let's just get to camp," she said, and set off walking without waiting for the others.

The rest of the party caught up eventually. Brit heard Lynx introduce Crux and Burgrave to Gemma and the other Citizens as they walked. She noticed that Lynx glossed over the fact that Crux and Burgrave were Altairi. After yesterday's showdown, that wasn't much of a surprise. Brit just hoped that no one recognized Burgrave or Crux, or they'd be in for more of the same.

The atmosphere of the Pyxian camp was different, even if the layout was the same. The Pyxians still arranged their tents in circles around a meeting area, but the outermost ring of tents was empty.

"In case we are attacked," Gemma explained. "Be careful to stay on the main path."

Brit was about to ask why when the question answered itself. Crux stepped off the path and the ground collapsed beneath him. It had just been a loose covering over a pit. Crux fell onto a sharpened stake. Had he been a character with a lower defense stat, the spike trap could have done a lot of damage. As it was, the stake collapsed under Crux's bulk.

"It's not a perfect system," Gemma explained as Crux clambered back up toward the others.

"Obviously not," Lynx agreed. "Come on. We need to call a meeting of everybody."

Gemma nodded and hurried off to issue summons.

"My tent is up ahead," Lynx said. "We can rest there until the meeting."

She led the way to a small tent near the center of the camp. But like many structures in Io, the tent was larger on the inside than the outside. Inside were enough chairs for everyone to sit down. Crux and Brit, too large for items made for normal NPCs, ended up standing, but Brit didn't mind. She felt too restless to sit down anyway.

After what felt like ages, Gemma reappeared and said the camp was assembled. As Brit exited the tent, she was shocked to see so many NPCs. The camp had been almost dead when they arrived, and yet there were at least two hundred Pyxians assembled in the center of the camp, with hundreds more gathered in the innermost rings of tents. Where had they all been? Brit wondered if they were all hiding in their tents, biding time until an invasion came.

Looking at the NPCs, it was hard to see them as anything but resigned to their fate. Brit couldn't blame them for that. They'd survived a war with the Altairi, and now they were in the middle of another conflict.

Lynx stepped forward and the crowd fell silent. Brit watched Lynx take in the entire crowd before she began to speak. She didn't envy the princess for having to explain the graying to her people.

"I bring great tidings, my people," Lynx said. "In my travels, I have found our champions from The Floating Eye, Brit and Mikayla!"

The Pyxians cheered. Brit hadn't realized how big her legend had grown in Pyxis, but maybe the Citizens were aching for some kind of savior. They stomped their feet and applauded with all their might. But Brit couldn't shake the thought that three of the champions from The Floating Eye should have been there. The applause of NPCs couldn't fix her guilt over Suzanne.

Lynx waited for the crowd to finish before continuing. "With their help I hope to strike back against those who have corrupted our land."

"Death to Leo!" an NPC yelled.

"No!" Lynx cried. "No. That is not our way. He is my brother and he has been misguided, but we do not kill our own. No, we must strive to restore sanity to our land."

This was met with further mutterings from the crowd, but Lynx cleared her throat and they fell silent. When she spoke again, her tone was deadly serious.

"Fellow Pyxians," she said. "I have grave news. A terrible change is coming across our land, transforming our people into monsters."

Instantly, panicked voices broke out in the crowd.

"How is that possible?"

"This must be a ploy of Ramses!"

"We aren't safe! None of us are safe!"

Alphonse banged his axes together until the crowd was silent once more.

"These creatures can be defeated. Like any other invader, we will drive them from our land," Lynx shouted. "We must be brave! We must not let ourselves give into our fear."

"Easy for you to say! You got your fancy weapons and your guards!" yelled a voice in the crowd. Brit scanned the faces for the NPC who had spoken, but she couldn't discern them among the masses.

Other voices spoke up, adding their complaints to the first. A second wave of NPCs began to argue with the first, calling them cowards and traitors. Lynx was losing control of the crowd. Brit figured the NPCs were afraid and lashing out for someone to blame.

Mikayla caught Brit's eye. Brit knew what she was thinking. There was no way this rabble could stand up against the forces of Xenos. The smarter move might be to cut their losses and split while they still could.

Brit felt someone tapping her on the shoulder. It was Mallon.

"You've got to speak to them," she said. "They need some encouraging."

"Me? They won't even listen to Lynx," Brit whispered. But if Lynx could hear her over the crowd, she gave no sign. She was deep in conference with Alphonse while the NPCs argued among themselves.

"You're a hero," Mallon shrugged. "That's got to count for something."

Mikayla was listening, and she nodded. "You trained all those NPCs in Zenith City," she said. "Just try to calm them down." She smiled at Brit, and Brit knew she couldn't let Mikayla down.

She stepped in front of the crowd. "Gimme a hand,

Crux," Brit said. Crux nodded. With mailed fists, he beat on his chest like it was a drum. The two large Dragoons, one banging on his chest plate, were enough to quiet the crowd. The Pyxians stared at Brit expectantly.

Brit hesitated. What could she say? The NPCs were probably screwed, but she obviously couldn't tell them that. But she could see them getting uneasy again, so she took a deep breath and shouted: "Just chill the fuck out!"

That shut them up.

"We, uh, we're here to help!" Brit shouted. "Lynx didn't tell you all the full of it. These creatures—it's Xenos who's doing it. He's the same asshole who corrupted Leo. He's even the one who pushed Ramses into the war."

"I won't lie to you," Brit continued. "He's a scary dude. He's done some scary shit. But there's only one of him, and there are so many of us. So if we stay strong, if we stay together, maybe we can beat him?"

"Maybe?" a voice cried from the crowd. "Maybe we can beat him?"

"Yeah," Brit replied. "Maybe. I won't lie to you and say we're going to stomp him, because we aren't. He's got at least one army on his side. And we don't know everything he's capable of. But here's the thing: he doesn't know how badass you all are. I mean, you're Citizens, but I can see that you've been handling your shit. So who cares how tough Xenos is? We've got this."

She could see each Pyxian arguing with their neighbor. At least they weren't about to come to blows.

"What are you doing?" Lynx hissed. Brit turned around to see the princess scowling at her.

"I'm just trying to help out," Brit said.

"I'm in charge here," Lynx said.

"What's your issue?" Brit asked. "Seriously. You're beginning to sound a lot like your brother. We're all on the same side, okay?"

"Are we?" Lynx asked. "Or are you and Mikayla just trying to help yourselves, like always?"

"What's that supposed to mean?" Brit said. Behind her she could hear the crowd growing restless again.

"Ever since you first arrived in Pyxis, you've only been interested in your own goals. Even when you fought with us in the war it was only so Libra would rebuild the Queen's Vault. I just don't know what you stand to gain out of all this."

"Besides staying alive?" Mikayla asked, her hands on her hips. "Seriously, Lynx, you should be thanking us. You were about to have a riot on your hands."

Lynx was about to yell back, but she stopped, her mouth hanging open from shock. Brit realized the crowd had fallen silent again. Following Lynx's gaze, she saw a lone NPC walking slowly through the outer rings of camp.

The bright red cape draped over his shoulders was in tatters. His fine robe was ripped as well, like he had been traveling nonstop. He limped along, supporting himself with a tall staff. As he neared the edge of the crowd, the NPC stumbled but caught himself.

"Holy shit," Brit said. "What the hell is Leo doing here?"

Chapter 6

"All I am is sorry," Leo said. He had always been an earnest-looking NPC, wide-eyed in his love for his country. Even when he was a puppet of Xenos, Xenos used Leo's desire to do right by his people to control the king. But now some of that earnestness was gone. In its place was a look of abject defeat.

Mikayla could hear the Pyxian mob buzzing outside. Leo had barely made it to the Pyxian camp before collapsing. Lynx ordered him taken to her tent where she could interrogate her brother. Mikayla, Brit, Alphonse, and Mallon were all invited inside. The rest of the camp pressed around the tent, eager for justice against a king they thought had betrayed them.

But whatever Leo had done, now he was a husk of his former self. His strident confidence was gone along with his crown.

He held his face in his hands as he spoke. "My people . . . no, our people, I have failed them. A calamity has struck the Capital. With our walls and our moats, I thought we were safe, but this was no enemy with sword or spear. The Citizens, they . . . they have changed. They are monsters. I barely made it out of the city."

Mikayla felt a thrill of fear. If the graying had spread to New Pyxia, how long until it reached the Pyxian camp? But that seemed like the last matter on Lynx's mind.

"You betrayed your people!" she said, her voice rigid with fury. "You sold them out to an Altairi, and for what? For a promise of a prettier throne? A grander capital?"

Leo shook his head and sank lower into his chair. "I can't say what came over me. But when the change happened, it was like I was waking up. I went to expel

Xenos personally, but he was already gone. My court attacked me and I fled, leaving any others unchanged to those creatures who had been our people."

Lynx crossed her arms. "That makes two times you have abandoned our people, then. Even if you were not a traitor, you are a coward."

"I am your brother," Leo said.

"That is all you are," Lynx replied. "You were never fit to rule, I see that now. You are no longer king of Pyxis. Swear your allegiance to me and I will not let the Citizenry outside tear you apart."

What the hell is she doing? Mikayla thought. She thought Leo was gone beyond saving, but looking at him now she wasn't sure. Not that she could ever trust him again, but Leo was in a pathetic state. He wasn't a danger to any of them. And who knows, maybe his healing could be useful.

But she didn't know if Lynx would listen to her. Surrounded by her own people, Lynx seemed even less flexible than before.

Alphonse stood behind Lynx, his hands on his axes.

Mallon was seated beside her. The Adept looked as unforgiving as his self-appointed queen. Beside Lynx was Mallon, who watched Lynx with sad eyes. Of all the Pyxians, only Mallon seemed to really understand that there was more at stake than the pride of a kingdom.

Maybe Mallon could see what Mikayla was seeing. Lynx was spiraling, just as her brother had spiraled. She should have been pressing Leo for details about New Pyxia, trying to find out how exactly the graying had affected the Capital. Instead, she was consolidating her power.

Mikayla had been feeling uneasy about Lynx ever since she blew up at Burgrave. And when she yelled at Brit at the assembly, Mikayla suspected Lynx was just trying to preserve her own influence. Her grandstanding was just more evidence that Lynx was becoming more like Leo . . . more like Ramses.

Mikayla wondered how Libra had been such a good queen. Power seemed to corrupt every NPC who received it, including both of Libra's siblings. Maybe

Ramses had taken his throne as an altruist, but his time ruling made him want more and more power. Only Libra had seemed like a just ruler, listening to the advice of her counselors, but not letting any one of them unduly influence her.

"Swear it," Lynx was saying. "Swear your loyalty now."

Mikayla saw Brit frown, but she didn't say anything. Mallon looked away from the siblings.

"No," Mikayla said.

Lynx sighed. "This is not the time for you to interfere," she spat. "This is a Pyxian affair. I appreciate all you and Brit have done for my people, but if you are to stay here you will need to listen to my law."

Brit's eyes flashed a warning, but Mikayla knew what she had to do. It was something she should have done months ago.

"You aren't the queen," Mikayla said, struggling to keep her voice level. "Before she died, Libra asked me to succeed her."

Both Lynx and Leo stared at Mikayla with wide

eyes. Brit's mouth hung open with shock. Only Mallon seemed unfazed by Mikayla's revelation. Mikayla thought she saw a faint smile on the elder NPC's face.

Lynx laughed. "What are you talking about? Libra would never give the throne away to a stranger."

But Libra had. She had deduced that Mikayla wasn't from Io at all, but from what the Pyxians called the higher realm, what Mikayla thought of as reality. Libra thought someone from that realm, someone with Mikayla's perspective would be a better ruler than any NPC. And maybe, Mikayla realized, maybe Libra had been right all along.

"Libra picked me," Mikayla repeated. "She saw something in me that convinced her I would do right by your people, and I will. Look at yourself, Lynx! You're ranting about your right to rule and swearing allegiance, but your people are turning into monsters! What does it matter if Leo swears loyalty to you? Right now we need to figure out a way to stop Xenos. Leo's the one who's spent the most time with that freak and instead of trying to get answers from him, you're embarrassing him."

"Even if your ludicrous story is true," Lynx began. Mallon cut her off. "It is," she said.

"What?" Lynx was nearly shouting now.

"Your sister told me herself. Near the end, but you know Libra. She was lucid until the last. She said Mikayla had it in her to be an even better ruler than she was. See us through the war, and even more, see us into peace."

Mallon turned toward Mikayla and said, "I wish you'd said something back when we were choosing a successor. Would've saved us all a lot of pain."

"Have you all gone mad?" Lynx cried. "I am the queen now. I am the one who has been fighting for our people while you," she pointed a finger at Leo, "abandoned them to Xenos and you," she gestured toward Mikayla, "tried to leave our land forever! Whatever Libra might have believed, too much has happened since then. You cannot simply claim the right to rule now that it suits you!"

She isn't wrong, Mikayla thought, but that didn't diminish her conviction. "Leo isn't king anymore," Mikayla said. "You want to be the next queen of Pyxis when this is all over, fine, we can talk about that then. But we need to take out Xenos before he turns everyone into one of those creatures. That's what matters right now, and you don't seem to get that."

"You got us this far," Mallon said gently. "But if we want to do this proper, if we want to vote on a successor, then Mikayla is my pick."

Lynx looked from Mikayla to Mallon, searching for some doubt. But Mikayla saw none in Mallon's face and felt none herself. This was the way forward. This was how they were going to beat Xenos.

"The people will never follow her," Lynx said weakly.

"I don't know," Brit said. "If they would listen to me then they're going to listen to Mikayla."

Alphonse drew his axes and stepped out from behind Lynx's chair. "I hardly think we need the opinion of more foreigners."

Mikayla saw pity in the way Brit looked at Alphonse. "Put them down, Al," she said. "You really don't want to start this."

"You do not command me!" Alphonse roared.

Brit grabbed her halberd out of her inventory.

"No!" Leo shouted. "No, we cannot fight among ourselves. This is what he wants! If we destroy each other, who will oppose him?"

No one spoke. Mikayla saw Lynx staring at her brother. Her anger from earlier was gone. In its place was a glimmer of recognition.

"Alphonse," Lynx said softly. The Adept turned to regard his queen. "They may be right."

She cleared her throat and stood. She withdrew her naginata from her inventory. Mikayla's hand went to the hilt of her sword, but Lynx bent and laid her weapon at Mikayla's feet. "Until we end Xenos once and for all. Until he is but pixels and no trace remains. Until then, I will follow you."

To Mikayla, Lynx sounded like she was pronouncing her own death sentence. But if they were going after Xenos then that might have been exactly what she was doing.

Alphonse looked like he was about to choke, but he kept his silence. Leo sagged back into his chair. Mallon's smile remained thin.

But Brit was beaming. And that was all the support Mikayla needed.

"Okay," she said. "Mallon, go grab Burgrave and Crux."

Mallon nodded and left the tent.

"Where is Suzanne?" Leo asked quietly.

Mikayla flinched at the sound of Suzanne's name. Of course, Leo didn't know.

"She's gone," Brit said. "Gemini did it."

Leo looked from Brit to Mikayla like he hoped Mikayla would say Brit was joking, that Suzanne was right outside waiting to surprise him. And Mikayla wished Brit was joking. As it dawned on Leo that it was all true, that Suzanne was indeed gone, his face crumpled.

Mikayla wasn't surprised by how aggrieved Leo

was. He had never stopped loving Suzanne with the same single-mindedness he applied to everything. But Mikayla was surprised to see her own desolation reflected in the Pyxian's eyes. She had never expected to feel so much sympathy for an NPC, and she had never expected an NPC to feel as deeply as she did.

He sat with his head hung until Burgrave and Crux arrived. The Altairi bowed as they entered. Mallon must have informed him of the regime change on the way to the tent.

"You called for us?" Burgrave asked.

"Yes," Mikayla said, tearing her eyes away from Leo. They could all mourn later. Tonight, they would plan a war.

Chapter 7

"You should have told me," Brit said. She didn't want to sound pissed because she wasn't.

She and Mikayla were in their tent. The meeting with the NPCs had gone on for another hour and a half as Mikayla laid out what the new responsibilities would be. For Brit, it was bizarre seeing Mikayla take charge like that, but she couldn't think of anyone in Io she trusted more to do the job.

Now, Brit was pushing their cots together so they formed something approximating a queen-sized bed. *A queen bed for a queen*, Brit thought.

Mikayla removed her armor and sat down on the bed. "I didn't think it would ever come up," she said.

"When Libra called for me on The Floating Eye, I just thought it was weird, you know? Like why would she want to talk to me? But she knew we weren't NPCs."

"What?" Brit had respected Libra as much as she could respect an NPC, but she never thought the queen, or any other NPC, would ever realize the truth.

"Yeah," Mikayla agreed. "It was freaky. She told me she wanted me to be the next queen and then she died. And when we left Pyxis, I figured that was the end of it."

"Still," Brit said. "You should've told me."

Mikayla shrugged. "You wouldn't tell me about your dreams. How's this any different?"

"I don't know," Brit said. "But it is different. And besides, I told you about my dreams eventually. You know, it just took a while is all."

Mikayla rolled her eyes. "I had to make you tell me."

Brit laughed. "Yeah, I guess so."

She lay down next to Mikayla. Laughter bubbled up in Brit.

"What's so funny?" Mikayla asked.

"If you're the queen, then that makes me your consort."

Mikayla laughed. "SAT word," she said.

"Oh my god. I can't believe you would bring that shit up."

"Okay," Mikayla said. "Okay, you have to pick. Take the SAT or fight Xenos one on one."

Brit screwed her face up, pretending to be deep in thought. "Can I copy off someone if I choose the SAT?"

"No. You have to take it locked in a dungeon."

"I'd fight Xenos. He might actually kill me, but at least I won't die a slow death from boredom."

She laughed, but she realized Mikayla had stiffened.

"Don't joke about that," she said.

"Sorry," Brit began, but Mikayla cut her off.

"Seriously. That isn't funny. I wouldn't be doing any of this if it wasn't for you. I'm going to keep you safe."

Mikayla looked so fierce Brit couldn't help but

believe her. Brit leaned forward and kissed her. Whether or not they would be okay, at least they were going to make it through this night.

"And then we'll live happily ever after, queen and queen consort?" Brit asked.

"Something like that," Mikayla said.

Brit looked at Mikayla's face. It wasn't really Mikayla, she knew, just an avatar made to resemble her. In reality, Mikayla's lips were bigger, her nose flatter. Her eyes weren't violet, but they also weren't monochromatic like a player character's. It was going to be like starting over, once they got out of here. But that was an exciting thought for Brit.

Mikayla reached over and extinguished the torch in their tent. In the darkness, as she fell asleep, Brit tried to remember what her own face looked like. *It's going to suck being so short again*, Brit thought, as she drifted off to sleep.

Brit smelled erasers and sat up. The glare of fluorescent lights bounced off the linoleum tiles. Students sat in desks and chairs older than they themselves were.

"Remember," Mr. Wells was saying, "even if you don't know the answer, don't stress out. You can always retake the test."

Brit blinked. Mr. Wells was the Intro to Tech teacher. He never gave tests. As he set the heavy packet down on Brit's test she saw SAT stamped clearly on the front.

Well, shit, Brit thought. She reached down into her bag and felt around for a pencil, but her bag was completely empty. She turned to her neighbor to ask to borrow one, and Brit nearly fell out of her seat.

It was Suzanne.

"What the fuck?" Brit said.

"Brit!" Mr. Wells yelled from the front of room. "Watch your language! And no talking, the test has begun."

He turned around and wrote the end-time of the current section of the test on the chalkboard.

Brit watched him for a second until she was sure she was in the clear. "What the fuck?" she hissed to Suzanne, who smiled and handed her a pencil.

Brit looked at the pencil like she had never seen one. "Forget the pencil! How the hell are you here?"

"This is the only day they're doing the SAT here," Suzanne replied. "Otherwise I'd have to go over to Towson to take it."

Brit resisted the urge to smack her. "That's not what I'm talking about! I saw you die! What the hell happened to you?"

Suzanne glanced up at the chalkboard. "You're going to run out of time," she said.

"Who gives a shit about this test? Tell me what's going on!"

"If you're confused," Suzanne whispered, "then you should try reading the instructions."

She buried her nose in her test. Brit sighed and flipped hers open and began to read the first page:

If Suzanne had the key to the Oracle Chamber, and Suzanne was killed in a fight, then what happened to the key? A) The key was destroyed, B) A weremonkey has it, C) Gemini took the key from a loot drop, or D) Ramses's ghost stole the key.

What the fuck? Brit thought. She glanced over at Suzanne's scantron and saw that Suzanne had circled *C*. Brit circled in *C* on her answer sheet, and as she did the little bubble began to glow.

Brit and Mikayla need to find Gemini, the next question read. *But they don't know where to find her. Is Gemini in A) The Fenlands, B) Zenith City, C) Vale, or D) Oppold?*

Brit looked over at Suzanne, whose head was buried in her test. Her shoulders were now positioned so Brit couldn't see any of her answers. "Suzanne!" she whispered loudly.

Suzanne raised a finger to her lips. "*Shh!* You're going to get us in trouble."

Brit was about to argue back when she saw Mr. Wells staring her at her from the front of the room.

Turning back to her own test, Brit looked over the answers again. The last time she had seen Gemini was in Pyxis, and Vale was the only answer that was in Pyxis, so she began to circle the bubble in. But as she did, the bubble began to glow red. A large thunk sounded, the same noise that happened whenever one of the girls attempted an illegal game action.

Brit hastily flipped her pencil over and began to erase her answer. So Gemini wasn't in Vale, then where was she? Her next guess was the Fenlands and that was also wrong. But when Brit tried *B*, for Zenith City, the bubble glowed white.

The next question asked, *Who is Xenos?*

A) Elias, B) Henny, C) Russell, D) None of the Above, or E) All of the Above

It couldn't be answer *E*, Brit knew that much. From a logical standpoint that didn't make sense. Well, Suzanne probably knew the answer. But when Brit looked up from her test, Mr. Wells was standing right in front of her.

Only it wasn't Mr. Wells. It was Xenos. Brit

dropped her pencil in surprise and it clattered to the floor. The long hood of his purple robe obscured his face as always, and when he spoke, it was in the same mechanical voice that always gave Brit a chill.

"Keep your eyes on your own paper," Xenos said. Instinctively, Brit motioned to open her inventory, but nothing happened when she tried. There wasn't even the thunk of an illegal game action.

She looked around her desk for a weapon. All she had was a pencil. At least that had a point.

Brit leaned over to grab her pencil. When she sat up Xenos was back in his seat across the room. And now she was alone in the room. All the other students were gone, and then the room was gone, as well, replaced by the stark stone walls of a dungeon.

"Finish your test, Ms. Acosta," Xenos commanded.

Brit pushed back her chair and made to stand up, but she realized her legs were chained to the desk. How had she not noticed that before? Then more chains sprang out of the walls and wrapped themselves around her wrists, slamming them back into the desk.

"Finish your test," Xenos repeated.

"Fine!" Brit shouted. She looked down and saw the fourth question.

What should Brit do? the question read.

The answers were: *A) Wake up, B) Wake up, C) Wake up, or D) Wake up.*

Brit circled *B*. She opened her eyes.

The pushed-together cots were rigid beneath her back. She rolled over and Mikayla wasn't there. Brit waited for her eyes to adjust to the low light of the tent, but Mikayla was nowhere to be seen.

She probably just went for a walk, Brit said. But her heart was racing. She needed to talk about what she had just dreamed. Suzanne was there—the real Suzanne—but what had happened to her? And those test answers—were they just more dream bullshit? The dream was like a bad song stuck in her head: impossible to forget, impossible to focus on anything else until it was exorcised.

Brit got out of bed and equipped her armor. She wasn't going to come up with the answer alone. She walked across the tent to the entrance flap as something gray and stony and feral came charging through and tackled her back into bed.

Brit shoved the Citizen off her and rolled off the other side of the bed. The creature leapt over the cots at her and Brit grabbed it mid-jump, throwing it into the canvas wall behind her. The creature ripped through the tent and crashed into the next tent over.

For a second, Brit was concerned about the Citizens in the next tent. But then the creature rose and threw back its head and gave a bloodcurdling scream. Two other figures rose out of the collapsed tent, both gray and clawed.

Brit looked to her left and saw more of the Citizens lumbering toward her. She grabbed her halberd out of her inventory as they surged forward.

Chapter 8

Mikayla hadn't gone to sleep when Brit did. She watched Brit sleep for a while. Brit mumbled something about test scores and Mikayla knew she was dreaming. Smiling, Mikayla left their tent.

The Pyxian night was cool and clear. Most of the Pyxians had gone to bed, and those still up were either heading home or moving about as sentries. Mikayla saw Burgrave sitting by the fire at the center of camp and steered clear. She didn't feel like talking to anyone right now.

Leaves crunched under her foot as Mikayla slipped out of the camp, past the Citizen sentries. She wished it hadn't been so easy to get past them. They were so focused on the area surrounding the camp that Mikayla could have walked right up behind them and smacked them on the head without them noticing.

But what else could she expect from Citizens?

Mikayla realized that they were no longer just Citizens. They were her responsibility. When she had won the showdown with Lynx, she had assumed responsibility for all of the Pyxians. They would listen to her—she had seen that already—but could she help them? Or was she just going to lead them all into a war they couldn't possibly win?

Did Suzanne ever feel this responsible? Mikayla remembered when the three of them first got to the ruins of Pyxia. The Pyxian capital had been absolutely destroyed in the war with Altair. Suzanne had taken the devastation from the war personally, seeing it as a failure of Io.

Back then, Mikayla had been too overawed by the destruction to argue with her. Instead, she and Brit tried to console Suzanne with the thought that once they left the game, Suzanne could fix everything she didn't like.

Now, when she thought about it, Mikayla wondered if Suzanne might have been wrong. Maybe the fact that the NPCs fought wars was a sign of the game's success. If they could care so passionately about things to fight over them, then maybe they were just like real people. The way Lynx humiliated Leo in front of the other Pyxians certainly reminded Mikayla of kids she knew in the real world.

The wind picked up, rattling the dry savannah. Off in the distance she could hear monsters crying. She took a deep breath and let the placidity of the night enter her body, letting herself breathe in time with the rushing of the wind. At times like this it was hard for her not to love Io.

She glanced back at the camp, the orange light of the central fire flickering over the tents. She thought about her NPCs—no, that was wrong. That was how Lynx and Leo thought, and Mikayla argued that she was better fit to lead than the siblings. The Pyxians weren't hers. She was helping them, guiding them at least until they dealt with Xenos.

What's going to happen after that? Mikayla couldn't know. But maybe, after Xenos was gone, she could return to New Pyxia and rule.

The first thing she would do would be to build a bridge connecting the castle to the rest of the city. Leo designed it so his castle was reachable only by ferry, but Mikayla would be an accessible ruler. Maybe she could start some kind of school or institute to work on developing new technologies. She pictured cars rumbling down the Grand Highway—the thought almost made her giggle—and electric lights in all the homes.

But was that even possible? Mikayla didn't know how long the TII would work. She didn't even know how long in game-time it would be until someone found their comatose bodies in the real world. After all, even with grassland reaching into the horizon, Mikayla was still sitting in Suzanne's room. She wasn't a Swiftblade or a queen. She was just a high school kid.

Maybe she and Brit could make it work. As long as Brit was with her she could stay sane in this crazy world. Mikayla thought about the gray icons that marked each and every NPC, and she knew that no matter what happened, those would always be there. These days the real world felt more like a memory than something waiting for her; yet, it was a strong memory, not one she could control.

Mikayla kicked a clump of grass and her foot snapped the brittle blades off of their roots. The grass pixelated. Even now, after all of these months in Io, Mikayla knew that wasn't natural. Or if it was natural for this world, it wasn't natural for her, no matter how much she might want it to be.

Then Mikayla heard a howl from the Pyxian camp.

Was Brit okay? Mikayla looked back at the camp and saw tents collapsing. She set off running at full speed. As she approached the outskirts of the camp, she drew her swords and her heart sank.

Where the sentries had been, only minutes earlier, were now two gargoyles. The creatures saw her coming, threw back their heads, and added their own cries to the chorus of howls.

Mikayla didn't slow down. She slid under the first gargoyle's claws, twisting around to stab it in the weak spot at the base of its neck. The second creature swiped at her, but she blocked and tripped it, sending it stumbling into a tent. As it stood back up, more of the creatures cut themselves free of the canvas. There were too many of them to fight so Mikayla sprinted past them to look for Brit.

Everywhere she looked there were gargoyles. Her tent—where she hoped Brit still was—sat on the other side of the fire, and Mikayla wasn't going to waste time finding a safe route around. She charged straight toward the center of camp, dodging what claws she could and watching her health bar drop when she couldn't get out of the way.

By the fire, his scimitar shimmering in the flames' light, she saw Burgrave holding off another horde. Crux came crashing out of the darkness and bulled into the creatures. Their claws scrabbled against his armor as his hammer smashed them to pixels. For a moment, the firepit was calm. But Mikayla could hear the cries of the creatures all around them in the darkness. There was no denying it. The camp had turned.

"Mikayla!" Burgrave said. "We need to leave this place."

"Not without Brit!" she shouted. Mikayla kept running past the Altairi, toward where her tent had been. Now there was just an empty space in the rows of tents, extending five tents in every direction. Brit fought two of the creatures in the center of the clearing.

All around her were little floating treasure chests, the loot drops from the Citizens Brit had already killed. There were at least twenty.

"Brit!" Mikayla yelled, and Brit turned around at the sound of her name.

Before Mikayla could call out a warning, another of the creatures materialized and drove its claws into Brit's back. Brit shouted in pain and elbowed the creature in the face until it was forced to the ground.

"Where the fuck were you?" Brit yelled.

"I'm sorry," Mikayla said. She vaulted over Brit and kicked another of the creatures, finishing it off as it fell to the ground. "Burgrave and Crux are back by the fire. Have you seen anyone else?"

"No," Brit said, knocking the head off of a gargoyle. Headless, the creature pixelated. "I was a little busy, you know?"

Mikayla almost laughed. They ran back to the fire where Crux and Burgrave were fighting a second wave of the creatures. Even as Brit and Mikayla joined the fray, more of the gargoyles came to reinforce their cohort. They flooded the circle around the fire, standing three deep. Crux and Brit struck gargoyles down but that didn't slow the other creatures at all. They were completely without pity or care for each other.

They encircled the party, driving them back toward the fire. Mikayla could feel the flames licking at her back. She thought back on the plans she had made earlier that night, for the war with Xenos and beyond. How stupid they now all seemed.

Then she heard an NPC cry, "Terraform!" and a

wall of earth burst up from the ground, blocking off the gargoyles.

"Follow me!" she heard Alphonse cry. Mikayla whirled around and saw him standing with Lynx, Leo, and Mallon on the far side of the fire. Alphonse swung his glowing axes into the ground again, spraying loam over the flames. Mikayla dashed forward over the smoldering fire pit with Brit beside her. As she ran, she grabbed one of the still-burning logs and hurled it at a tent.

"What are you doing?" Lynx cried.

"They're gone," Mikayla replied. "We can't help them. At least this way they won't follow us."

The log caught on one of the tents and began to burn. Soon the fire spread from tent to tent, ring to ring, until the entire camp was ablaze. As the party burst free of the camp, the Citizens threw back their heads and howled one more time. They were still howling when the flames consumed them.

Chapter 9

"The way ahead appears clear," Burgrave said.

Mikayla didn't respond. From her vantage point, half-covered by the thin woods, her eyes searched the riverside village for movement of any kind. What this town had once been was writ plainly in its ruins. She could see the remnants of an inn, one wall completely missing, standing near the town square. The thatched cottages still standing held the haunted aspect of abandoned homes. Its forge was still standing. A row of empty stalls, which must have been markets, backed into a small Oratorium.

One of the stalls rustled—it wasn't empty after

all—and out tumbled two hooting weremonkeys, playing at fighting.

Mikayla ignored them and kept looking. No doubt Burgrave had spotted them and deemed them unworthy of mentioning. Weremonkeys weren't a threat. At this point, none of the monsters populating the Pyxian countryside posed their party much of a threat. But the presence of the weremonkeys confirmed that the town was free of NPCs.

The weremonkeys noticed them and scampered off to somewhere with lower-leveled characters. Mikayla watched them go, concluding that the area around the shore of the Ion River was, as Burgrave had said, clear.

She turned to the diminutive NPC. "Seems good."

"If you would go fetch the others," he replied. "I will maintain the area."

Not waiting for an answer, he trotted out from the trees, his ruby earrings swishing. He drew his broad scimitar from its scabbard, sat down cross-legged in the town square, and lay the blade over his knees.

Was he meditating? Did NPCs even do that?

Mikayla pushed the questions out of her mind and turned back into the woods to find the others. It was easy enough to follow their own trail in reverse. Too easy. If anyone was following them, it wouldn't be hard to figure out where they had gone. There was an army chasing them, after all. But they wouldn't know how close that army was until the rear scouts, Mallon and Alphonse, came back with that intel.

Mikayla heard the rest of the party before she saw them. Well, not the whole party, but Brit.

"They're really taking their time, aren't they?" Brit said. Mikayla could picture the scowl on Brit's face as she said it. It was cute that Brit was worried—not that she'd ever admit it. But the louder Brit complained, the more she cared.

"I'm sure they'll be back soon," Mallon replied. Entering the clearing where the party waited, Mikayla saw Brit, Mallon, and Crux were seated in a circle. Lynx and Leo sat sullenly off to the side. Alphonse still hadn't returned from scouting out the rear.

"Hey," Mikayla said. Five heads whipped toward her. "We found a village up ahead. It looks okay."

Anything else she might have said was crushed out of her as Brit engulfed her in a bear hug.

"What about Alphonse?" Lynx asked. "Will he be able to find us?"

Leo put a hand on his sister's shoulder. "He's found us every other time. We just need to have a little faith."

Alphonse arrived in the abandoned town half an hour after the rest of the party. The news he brought was not good. The gargoyles had mobilized and were in pursuit of their party. Mikayla was already leading the party west to Altair, following Brit's dream. The reason she had given the NPCs was common sense: if the gargoyles were to the east, it made sense to get as far away from them as possible.

"We should cut south now and try to make it to the lily pad bridge," Burgrave suggested.

"There is no time," Alphonse replied. "Their line is so long that we are practically encircled already. Our only chance is to go east as soon as possible and hope these abominations cannot walk on water."

"And how do you suggest we do that?" Brit asked. "Unless you have a bunch of boats hidden in your inventory."

Leo laughed. "As a matter of fact, we do."

At dawn they were on the riverside, Brit tugging one of the boats and Crux the other. Leo and Lynx each owned a boat. Mikayla remembered riding in Leo's the first time she ever crossed into Pyxis. It seemed fitting that the same boat should ferry her away from Pyxis now.

Leo, Brit, and Mikayla rode with Mallon, leaving Alphonse and Lynx to ride with Crux and Burgrave. As soon as they set off, the current took them, dragging them into the center of the river. Mikayla hadn't remembered a current this strong in the Ion River. In her memories, the Ion was a lazy river, no wider than an arrow shot. This rushing river was nothing like that. For one thing, it was rushing. And for another, she hadn't seen the Archer that could clear the distance from one bank to the other.

"When did the river get rapids?" Brit yelled.

Mikayla was about to answer her. The boat lurched and she swallowed her words. A wave of water splashed over the side, drenching half of Mikayla's body.

"Seriously!" Brit said.

"Just shut up and hold on!" Mikayla said. The bow of their ship rose out of the water, slamming back down with a tremendous splash.

Right before the river wrapped around a bend, Mikayla saw the gargoyles arrive on the Pyxian shore. There were hundreds of them. Mikayla wondered if Xenos had transformed every village in Pyxis. They ran along the shore after the boat, but the Ion River's current outpaced them. A few swiped at the air over the river, and Mikayla exhaled a sigh of relief. The creatures could not, after all, swim.

But the moment of relief was fleeting. Mikayla gripped the sides of her boat, trying to hold on as it bucked over the rapids. She glanced back and saw Lynx's boat was having the same trouble. Up ahead on the Altairi side, the river bed rose into a sandy shore. "Lean left," she said. Brit threw her weight left immediately, almost tipping them. But they figured out the balance soon enough, and between the four of them managed to guide the boat toward the Altairi shore.

They moved more slowly once out of the middle of the river. Leo and Mallon took two of the oars and used them like rudders, turning the boat toward shore at a sharper angle. Mikayla looked back at the other boat and saw them turning the same. The beach they aimed toward was wide enough for both boats to dock. To Mikayla, it looked perfect.

Then a bush moved. Its leaves shook and then stopped too suddenly. Mikayla knew it wasn't a monster. Monsters would keep at whatever they were doing and the rustling would continue. Whatever was in the bushes was trying to hide. It had given itself away.

"Something's over there," she called to Brit, and again, Brit didn't hesitate. She whipped a throwing axe at the bushes. There was a clank as the axe-blade hit the bush and bounced off whatever was hiding there.

Mikayla saw it first, of course, but by then everyone in the boat could guess what it was. Clawed hands, like the gray stone of a gargoyle, parted the bushes as a transmogrified Citizen rose from its hiding place. The creature was grotesque. Once upon a time it had been a normal Citizen, an NPC minding its own business, but it hardly bore any resemblance to a human now.

Its skin was like flint, its eyes yellow. Every corner of its body was an edge. A row of spikes protruded from its shoulders, jutting from its arms. That was new. Like these creatures weren't unpleasant enough already.

When Mikayla had first encountered them she hadn't known how to react. They were still close enough to NPCs then that she was paralyzed by what they had been. But now she had no such compunction.

"Back to the current!" she yelled. Mallon and Leo rowed back toward the current in the center. The creature picked up Brit's axe and lobbed it at the boat.

The throw missed by ten feet. But the sound of the splash was lost as the creature threw back its head and let loose a blood-curdling shriek. Without thinking, Mikayla's hands flew up to her ears, in an attempt to block out the sound. Mallon and Leo did the same, dropping their paddles. The bits of wood drifted away on a current. They were now at the mercy of the river, Mikayla realized, but it was hard for her to focus on anything except the former Citizen's screeching.

"Someone shut it up!" Brit yelled.

But how could they? Still, the creature howled. "What's it doing?" Leo asked.

"Calling for friends," Mallon answered. Mikayla followed the NPC's gaze to the foliage behind the creature. One after another, dozens of the creatures emerged from the bushes. Had they been waiting there all this time? It wasn't like the creatures to show patience. And they stood on the shore, neatly lined up, almost in formation—they looked less like a horde and more like an army. Another thought occurred to Mikayla. With their stony complexion, the mass of creatures resembled something else: a wall. One that their party had no chance of breaking through.

"Holy shit," Brit said.

"Holy shit," Mikayla agreed.

"We cannot land here!" Lynx's boat had pulled level with the girls'. The princess was leaning out of her boat, her hands cupped around her mouth as she shouted the obvious at them.

"What's the plan, then?" Brit called back.

"Keep heading south," Lynx replied. The current pushed her boat away. Mikayla saw Alphonse grappling with a makeshift rudder, trying to steer the two boats back together, but the river was too strong. Lynx's boat drifted back toward the Pyxian shore, while Mikayla's stayed east of the current, closer to Altair.

South it was, though to Mikayla it hardly seemed like they had a choice in the matter. The current was carrying them now. The river ride was almost pleasant: cool spray splashed up into the boat, and while strong, the current was steady, carrying them at an even pace. Yet menace permeated the scene, considering the creatures. The wall of creatures stretched on and on, baleful yellow eyes lining the river. It was unsettling, but Mikayla reminded herself that the creatures still couldn't swim. She leaned back into the boat, trying her best to ignore them.

Brit made that difficult. "How'd they know where we were going?" she asked. "We didn't even know where we were going!"

Mallon didn't take her eyes off the shore. "Seems likely that Xenos got word ahead of us somehow."

"Help!" Burgrave's voice was no longer monotone, but sharp with panic.

She snapped to attention and saw his cause for alarm. A huge ship was barreling down the river toward them. How had she missed it? Even if she was looking forward, she should have heard the crash of the ship. She could certainly hear it now. Mikayla looked further, willing her enhanced awareness to work.

A roaring lion served as the figurehead, leaning out from the prow, snarling at the waves. Lining the deck behind the ship were more of the transmogrified Citizens. But they weren't just waiting, like their kin on the Altairi side. The Citizens on deck adjusted rigging and performed other tasks of a crew.

On a lower deck of the ship, oars were poking through slats and sinking into the water. Just how many of the creatures were on board? Manning the ship's wheel was a huge gargoyle, bigger than any other Mikayla had seen.

"Where did they get a warship?" Mikayla shouted.

Leo looked particularly miserable at that moment. "I had been working on it," he said, "to protect the river against Ramses. Xenos said it was a wise countermeasure."

"We'll never outrace him!" Mallon shouted. "We've got to get off the water."

Before they could move, the ship's figurehead shot forward. A chain connected it to the gargoyles' warship. Like a wildcat pouncing on its prey, the jaws of the lion head sank into the rear of Lynx's boat. Alphonse jumped out of the way just in time to avoid damage, but the back of their dinghy exploded, throwing debris into the air that pixelated before hitting the waves.

Three of the creatures on deck produced a winch and began recoiling the chain, dragging Lynx's dinghy back toward Leo's warship. The current broke against the dinghy as it skipped backwards over the waves.

Mallon was first to act. "Hey Crux!" she shouted. "Catch!" Her silver whip uncoiled like a living thing and lashed out. Crux extended an arm—that was enough. Mallon's whip coiled around Crux's arm.

She shoved the handle of the whip into Brit's arms. Brit didn't need to be told. She pulled the whip taut.

Three Citizens were no match for Brit's strength. It was unfortunate that there were more than three Citizens. Others broke off from manning the rigging to help turn the winch, others leaning overboard and grabbing onto the chain. Groaning, the winch turned another rotation and the dinghy scooted another half-foot back toward the warship.

Brit was pulled up to standing. Mikayla wrapped her arms around Brit, felt Leo grab her by the shoulders. In the other boat, Alphonse, Lynx, and Burgrave were holding onto Crux. The tug of war continued as both chain and whip tautened.

Like a leaf on the wind, Lynx's dinghy rose out of the water. More and more Citizens were joining the hauling team, the winch was turning faster and faster. Mikayla felt the boat shift beneath her feet. With panic she realized that they were all going to go overboard if they didn't let go.

Then Alphonse rose. Without his strength, the whip slid another inch forward, pulling Mikayla along with it.

"What's he doing?" Leo shouted. No one answered him. No one needed to do. Alphonse's actions spoke loud enough.

Like a tightrope-walker he climbed up onto the chain. Steadying himself, an axe in each hand, he ran forward onto the warship.

He vaulted over the railing feet-first, kicking two

of the Citizens off the winch. He landed on his back, springing back to standing and swinging his axes like cudgels to knock another Citizen off. The creatures—at least, the ones already on the winch—ignored him and kept turning it.

More came up from below decks. Hissing, they charged Alphonse with their claws extended.

The first and second he knocked overboard, but the third was on him before he could prepare himself, and the fourth, fifth, and sixth buried him in a dog pile.

For a second, Mikayla lost sight of him. Her heart sank. The next second he erupted from the dog pile, scattering the Citizens. Mikayla could see his knees shaking, his shoulders heaving with each breath he took. And still the winch turned another link.

Alphonse's axe-blades glowed. A claw raked at his gut and he leapt back out of range, back up onto the rail. Then he threw himself up into the air—up and forward—and brought down his axes like judgment on the deck of the ship.

It was hard for Mikayla to follow what happened

next. Alphonse's blow tipped the entire warship forward, its prow dipping beneath the water. Its deck exploded, throwing Citizens and wood from the ship in every direction. The winch tumbled overboard, pixelating. Lynx's dinghy slammed back into the water, and a wave rose from the point of impact, shoving both dinghies, still bound together by the whip, far south of it all.

"Alphonse!" Lynx screamed. She moved toward the aft of her boat, but Crux grabbed her before she did anything desperate. The princess strained against the Dragoon for a moment before she gave up and fell back into the boat. Whatever else she shouted in her grief was lost beneath the rushing river.

They left the warship behind them—how could they not? They left Alphonse behind them as well. Mikayla thought she had seen half a smile flicker on the Pyxian's face right before his axes connected. Though she might have invented that detail to make herself feel better about what had happened.

Chapter 10

"What do you see?" Brit asked. She was flat on her stomach, lying on the slope of the hill. Off in the distance, Zenith City's four pillars towered over the horizon. The sun had moved to the west, casting the whole area east of the Altairi capital in a cool shadow.

Mikayla was lying next to Brit. They were scouting—or Mikayla was, at least. Brit was with her because Brit wasn't going to let Mikayla out of her sight. Lynx had begun to argue that point before Brit made it clear that certain things were now inarguable.

The last few days had been non-stop travel but were still tremendously slow for Brit's taste. They slept in the woods, starting fires only when they absolutely needed to. They ended up much further south in Altair than they had intended, landing nearly at the Fens.

Brit didn't mind roughing it—she figured more than half her time in Io had been roughing it, one way or the other—but there was a mechanical, routine aspect to these days that began to wear on her. Wake up, pack up camp, scout ahead, get the others, set up camp, sleep, repeat . . .

They were going as fast as they could, but they had to stay off the Grand Highway. When they reached Altair's main road, the party had seen a seemingly endless line of CitiZombies marching north. Brit had tried to count their numbers, but she lost track somewhere around three hundred. She hoped that they weren't all headed to Zenith City, but she had no idea where else they could be going.

So the party waited for a break in the line and sprinted across the Grand Highway. Sticking to forest paths, they headed north to the Capital. And now they had reached Zenith City. That was where Brit's dream had said they would find Gemini. With any luck, they were going to catch their enemies unaware. No way Xenos would expect them to come marching right at him, right? Brit rolled over onto her back and stared up at the copy-and-pasted clouds dotting the blue sky.

Mikayla was sitting cross-legged on the top of the hill. She didn't need to hide herself like Brit did. Even if someone from Zenith City spotted Mikayla, she could be mistaken for just another NPC. Someone Brit's size meant trouble and would be reported no matter what. At least that's what Burgrave had said.

Brit watched Mikayla's head pan back and forth. "Well?" she asked. "What's up?"

To Brit's surprise, Mikayla was chuckling. "You're not going to believe this."

"What?" Brit demanded as Mikayla broke out into full-on laughter.

"Remember those Citizens you trained?"

The Zenith Citizens' guard had worked. After Ramses had lost his throne, monsters had begun to attack Zenith City. Normally, monsters wouldn't go near NPC settlements, especially not ones as big as Zenith City, but the game stripped the Capital of that protection. Brit and Mikayla had taken it upon themselves to train the able Zenith Citizens into a militia so they could defend themselves. The results had been laughable at the time.

But now things were different, Mikayla reported. Classed NPCs were massed around the entrances to Zenith City. A barricade manned by the Citizen militia kept them out. According to Mikayla, the militia was armed with nothing more than wooden weapons, makeshift spears from broom handles, shields from the tops of barrels and crossbeam swords.

"You're right," Brit said. "I can't believe it."

"They were so hopeless!" Mikayla laughed. "I mean, remember what Suzanne . . . " her voice trailed off as the laughter died in her eyes.

"Let's go tell the others," Brit said. The answer was to keep moving so the grief couldn't catch up to them.

They descended into a valley which wound around into the woods where the rest of the party waited. Brit counted to a hundred, counting her breaths and her steps, seeking solace in the mundanity of basic human upkeep. Or basic character upkeep, as it were.

After an appropriate pause, she asked Mikayla, "Did you see any CitiZombies?"

"Any what?"

"The Citizen-monster things. CitiZombies."

"Did you come up with that yourself?"

"Who else would have? Crux?"

Mikayla offered a fleet smile. *I'll take it*, Brit thought. *That's as much as I'm gonna get.*

"No," Mikayla said, "I didn't see any CitiZombies. Just a bunch of Paladins and Fighters and Sellswords trying to get through the barricade."

"Weird," Brit said. If there weren't any gargoyles, did that mean that Xenos wasn't in Zenith City? She didn't share her concern with Mikayla. They were only going to Zenith City because of Brit's dream, and Brit knew that wasn't much to go on. It wasn't like they had much info about Xenos, but one thing they did know was that Xenos had a longstanding interest in the

Oracle Chamber. The only Oracle Chamber remaining was in Zenith Castle. And wherever Xenos was they were likely to find Gemini.

As they crossed into the woods, Brit concluded that even though the logic was sound, nothing guaranteed it was right. Brit knew that, and Mikayla must have known too. *Shit*, Brit thought, *even Crux must be thinking it by now.* Not one of the party mentioned it. They were grasping at straws—no need to make that blatant.

"Stop moving." Mikayla's words cut the silence. Brit hadn't heard anything besides her own footsteps, but she froze anyway.

Mikayla cocked an ear to the west. "Get your weapon," she whispered, drawing her swords. Brit didn't need to be told twice. By now she could hear them crashing through the trees.

The gargoyles burst into view. They swarmed through the trees, claws scraping at bark. There weren't too many—just twenty. Completely manageable.

"That explains where they were," Brit muttered.

Mikayla didn't waste her breath on jokes. She was already engaging the nearest gargoyle, her two blades puncturing a dozen holes in its neck. It fell to the loamy earth with a groan and expired there. Mikayla chased after another one, vanishing behind a tree.

"Mikayla!" Brit called after her. A note of panic trilled within Brit, but she forced herself to ignore it. Mikayla could handle herself. Brit had to handle her own share of the fighting.

Brit slammed into a tree, knocking it off its roots onto a mass of the creatures. They tried to scatter, but not all of them made it out.

"Timber!" Brit yelled. Spinning on the spot, she hacked the legs out from another gargoyle, toppling it. She followed the momentum of her swing and planted her axe in a clavicle. The creature shrieked at her and twisted. Brit felt her halberd slip from her hands. She grabbed after it and missed, and just like that she found herself unarmed and surrounded by seven of the creatures.

The first one that leapt at her ate a knuckle

sandwich. The punch sent it sprawling backwards into a tree. Brit ran after it, slamming her elbow into its face, mashing its head repeatedly into the tree trunk.

The other six snarled and spat, clashing their claws against each other as they circled her again.

Brit waited for one to make a move, but they seemed just as content to wait as she was. She took a step forward and their circle adjusted to keep her in the center. The gargoyles moved in perfect unison, like they were guided by a single mind. Without a weapon, she couldn't reach them before they had time to move. And she couldn't throw herself at one of them wildly or the others would jump her from behind.

"Come on!" she shouted, but if the creatures understood speech they gave no sign. She couldn't stand here all day. She had to check on Mikayla and tell the rest of the party to move before reinforcements showed up. Oh, and also deal with these gargoyles.

Brit lunged forward. Predictably, the circle shifted with her. But she took that moment to grab into her inventory. Her fingers closed around something metal, hard and flat. The blade of a halberd? She whirled around, swinging the item at the nearest creature.

The plate armor smacked the gargoyle right in the face. Contact rang the armor like a bell, Brit didn't keep the beatdown going but turned back to face the other creatures as they reformed their ranks.

I've never fought with armor before, she thought. Two-handed, she raised the breast plate over her head and advanced toward the creatures. She brought the armor down once, twice, six times, a dozen. The gargoyles could only be cut at joints like their neck or their knees, but you could bludgeon them anywhere. And, apparently, with anything. Only when the creatures were pixels did she stop to catch her breath and inspect the armor.

It was dented all over from the damage it had taken. Brit checked its hit points and saw that it was on the verge of collapsing. Though all dinged up, one thing remained unblemished: the Altairi insignia. Ramses's sigil was a four-pillared pedestal supporting a crimson orb. The insignia was stamped all over Zenith City, but Brit hadn't seen it in a long time. The last time she wore the armor she was still questing for Ramses. After that, she had stashed it in her inventory and forgotten about it completely until right now.

She heard Mikayla calling her name and stuck the armor back in her inventory, taking the time to make sure she withdrew an actual weapon this time. She found Mikayla in a nearby clearing.

"You know what I hate?" Mikayla asked.

"Gargoyles?" Brit guessed.

"No. Well, yeah, duh. But I hate how they just give us one XP per kill. How ridiculous is that?"

A lump formed in Brit's throat. This was the point where Suzanne would add that to her never-ending list of bugs to fix when they got back to reality. But now . . .

They made a small fire that night, for comfort more than anything else. Mikayla reported what she had scouted. Mallon, who had been scouting the rear and the area closer to the Grand Highway, reported that the army of gargoyles was at most half-a-day's journey behind them. She hadn't been able to see the end of their line.

"But if we can get behind that wall, we might be able to finish this before they overtake us," Mallon added.

"Who rules in this suburb?" Leo asked.

"There was a Citizen named Hawthorne who had gained influence," Burgrave replied.

"Hawthorne?" Brit laughed. "We go way back with that dude. If he's still in charge then we should be able to get in, no sweat."

All that remained for the party was to figure out how they would get past the NPC soldiers surrounding the city. Once they finalized a plan, it was late enough that no one felt like doing much of anything but getting to sleep.

Brit volunteered to take the first watch. As everyone else headed to their tents for the night, she said, "Tomorrow, we're going to Zenith City and we're going to end this." *At least, I hope so*, she thought. *I really fucking hope so.*

Chapter 11

The next morning, as they crested the hill and descended into the plains before Zenith City, Brit finally got a good look at the Capital. The suburbs of Zenith City ran all the way to the edge of the city's shadow, tall buildings jammed together to use every bit of space. For once, the narrow streets of the suburbs worked in the Citizens' favor. They had less to barricade that way.

Classed NPCs were clustered around the barricade in a dense scrum. Besides a few projectiles exchanged between the Citizens defending the barricade and the classed NPCs, the two parties were calm.

A Defender and a Sellsword passed Brit and Mikayla walking the other way.

"Good luck getting through that lot," the Defender grumbled. "Blasted Citizens seem to think there's no use for us anymore. Just goes to show you how unreliable they were all along."

Brit grunted. She hoped it sounded like commiseration. That seemed to be how the Defender took it as he trundled off after his Sellsword companion.

Soon Brit could hear a buzz of chatter from the clustered NPCs.

"We've been here a week already," a pot-bellied Archer groaned. "Let us through!"

"Ain't got no use for your kind in here," a voice called down from the barricade.

"We'll break through eventually," a Monk snarled. "And when we do, you better watch out. We've got reinforcements coming up from the south. You just wait. Those wood walls will burn nice and bright soon enough."

The Monk's words were met with general support

from the surrounding NPCs. A Rogue turned to see Brit and Mikayla approaching and hailed them over.

"You two part of the Southern Forces?"

"The what?" Brit blurted out.

The suspicious look the Rogue gave them filled Brit with regret for her words.

"We were stationed by the river," Mikayla answered. "Last orders we had said to head to the Capital so here we are."

Her words seemed to relax him. It helped that they were both decked out in Altairi gear, courtesy of Burgrave. Hopefully that would camouflage them until they could speak with whoever was on the wall.

"Here we all are," the Rogue laughed, "until the south gets off its ass and opens the doors for us."

"You can't break the barricade?" Brit asked.

"Not for lack of trying," the Rogue replied. "The Citizens did something to it. We can't figure it out, it doesn't make any sense."

"Mind if we have a go then?"

"Suit yourself," the Rogue said. As they walked

away, he called after them, "Don't say I didn't warn you though."

Brit heard the sound of hammering growing louder and louder. Pushing through the crowd of NPCs she found the source of the sound.

Two Defenders stood with their shields raised as a canopy. Projectiles rained down from the barricade, bouncing off the shields ineffectually. Beneath the canopy, a Fighter hacked at the barricade with an axe. But just as the projectiles bounced off the shield the axe bounced off the walls.

The Fighter swung again and again, making no progress. Throwing all his might into the blow, the axe slammed into the barricade, shattering on impact. Disgusted, the Fighter hurled the pixelating axe-handle at the ground. The two Defenders and the Fighter retreated out of range of the Citizens' projectiles.

As funny as Brit found their frustration, now wasn't the time for laughter. Her plan required for her to get close enough to the barricade to speak with the guards and ask them for Hawthorne. But they wouldn't be able to get anywhere near the barricade without at least fifty classed NPCs seeing them. And even if they got word to Hawthorne, it wasn't like he could just lower down a ladder.

"Up and over," Mikayla whispered. "Give me a boost."

"You're gonna be fast, right?"

Mikayla flashed a smile. "Of course."

They entered the no man's land. A few of the soldiers called after them, but Brit ignored them. Projectiles began to fly down from the barricade. Brit stepped in front of Mikayla as a bulwark and raised her arm to shield her face from the worst of it. They took small slivers off her health bar, but nothing she couldn't get back. At this point, she was more worried about her Altairi armor giving out.

"Close enough!" Mikayla shouted over the hail of projectiles.

Brit felt Mikayla's hand on her shoulders. She turned her back to the barricade. Interlocking her fingers, she made a foothold for Mikayla. Mikayla stepped up, pushing down on Brit's shoulders as Brit tossed Mikayla over her head.

Brit spun back toward the barricade and saw Mikayla's feet clear the top as a rock hit her square in the nose. She took a dazed half-step backwards, her arms over her face.

Then the projectiles stopped.

"Hey!" someone behind Brit shouted. One of the soldiers. "Hey, she got the other one over!"

"Why didn't we think of that?" the Fighter said, slapping one of the Defenders in the chest.

"Give us a hand!" It was the same Rogue as earlier. "I could do some damage. I just need a leg up!"

"Back off!" Brit shouted at them as they approached.

The Rogue lead the procession forwards, his arms spread wide as he tried to look reasonable. "Look, we're all on the same side here. Literally, I mean. And you can help us over!"

The crowd began to press closer and closer. Brit

grabbed her halberd out of her inventory and swung it back and forth, to keep them at a distance.

"What is going on?"

Brit never understood how Burgrave could project his voice so well without shouting. He made a majestic figure on top of the hill, only made slightly comical by the large Altairi helm on his head. Burgrave took his helm off. Sunbeams bounced off his head.

"Shove it, old man," one of the soldiers shouted. He was immediately cuffed by his neighbor.

"Don't you know who that is? That's Burgrave, you numbskull."

"Burgrave? Like Commander Burgrave?"

"The very one." Burgrave called down. He descended the trail, tailed by Crux. Mallon and Lynx were nowhere to be seen.

"Wait a minute," the Rogue said, "I heard Burgrave defected. I heard he stole something from the king and scampered off like a thief in the night."

"Watch your tongue," Crux said, pointing his massive hammer at the Rogue.

"No, that sounds right," the Fighter said. He produced another axe. "We'll be rewarded for capturing him, I figure."

A Defender shook his head in disbelief, stepping away from the Fighter. "Are you mad? You can't just attack the king's right hand based on rumors."

"These aren't rumors," the Rogue said. "Let's get them."

Half the soldiers turned and began to advance toward Burgrave. They hadn't taken two steps before Burgrave drew his sword.

"If you attack me I will defend myself. I hope those loyal to the king will do the same."

The other soldiers, the ones who hadn't moved, turned on their comrades. Brit could hardly believe it as they all began to fight each other. The Fighter's axe clanged off the Defender's shield as the soldiers devolved into chaos. Brit backed up to the barricade, her halberd at the ready, but the soldiers seemed content to fight each other and leave her completely alone.

Crux smashed an opening through the mob.

Burgrave shoved the helm back on and stepped daintily in his wake. The Fighter broke off from his fight and threw himself at Burgrave, but Burgrave's scimitar cut him down in three quick strokes.

"Thanks," Brit said to Crux and Burgrave when they reached her.

"It seemed you could use some assistance," Burgrave said. "Though I would be lying if I said I did not take enjoyment from watching these buffoons."

"Where's Mallon and Lynx?"

Burgrave pointed at one of the hills with his scimitar. "They are waiting for us to open the way."

Brit nodded, but she wasn't sure how well that was going to work out. Now that she was up close to the barricade she couldn't see any way for the wall to open. That was assuming Mikayla had reached Hawthorne and wasn't . . . No. Brit wasn't going to let herself even think like that.

The battle was thinning the soldiers out. Brit saw one of the Defenders go down, his shield shattered. The Rogue met his end at the point of the pot-bellied

Archer's arrows, who in turn was taken out by a Ranger with a spear.

"The great army of Ramses," Burgrave said, a note of sadness in his voice.

Brit was so engrossed in their battle that she didn't realize someone was calling her name. A pebble bounced off her head, snapping her back to attention. She looked up to see who had thrown it and was met with a leering, adolescent smile.

"You got bigger. It's gonna be hard to pull you up like that."

"Ib?" Brit said. "Is that you?"

"The very one!" the boy cackled. "Hold on a tick, we'll haul you up right quick."

The last time she had seen Ib, Hawthorne's grandson, he was a tiny kid—now he looked ten or twelve. Had they been in the game that long? Or was childhood development as weird as everything else in Io?

Brit chalked it up as another thing to ask Suze until she remembered that she couldn't.

But before she let that line of thought consume her,

a rope dropped down, with a loop on the end. Then another fell.

"Put your arms through and hold on," Ib called down.

Brit did as instructed. With a tug and a jolt she found herself rising in the air. They pulled her over the barricade, her legs slamming against its top, and deposited her in a heap on the walkway running the course of the barricade.

Brit took a second to collect herself.

"Where's Mikayla?" she asked Ib.

"Talking with gramps. Now help us pick up this lug. He's even bigger than you!"

Crux rose smiling over the barricade. When it was Burgrave's turn, the Zenith Citizens were too exhausted from hauling Brit and Crux, but Crux easily managed by himself.

Once Burgrave was over the battlement, Ib made for the stairs down.

"Let's move out," Ib said. The other Citizens, adult NPCs, listened to his words without hesitation.

"Wait," Brit said. "There are three more of us."

As she spoke a familiar silver whip flew up over the barricade wall. Brit grabbed it and held on. Lynx popped her head over the wall—followed by her brother, and then Mallon—coiling it up after herself.

"What did you do to all the soldiers?" Ib asked them, peering over the edge.

"That was my fault," Burgrave said, stepping forward and removing his helm again. He was hardly taller than Ib.

"That's Burgrave!" one of the adults said, lowering a makeshift spear at Burgrave.

"Ramses's man?" the other one replied. With a nod of confirmation there were two spears pointing at Burgrave.

"You do not want to try that," Burgrave said. Behind him, Crux flexed, a mountain of metal shifting.

"Burgrave's cool!" Brit said, motioning for Crux to back down. "He's cool," she repeated, speaking directly to Ib.

Ib searched her face, looking for a reason not to

trust her. Not finding one, he nodded and said to his troops, "Put those up. They won't do us any good anyway."

Burgrave dropped his helm over the side and put his scimitar away. This seemed to relax the Zenith Citizens just a little.

They took a narrow walkway down to street level. Brit looked back up at the barricade. From the inside it looked far less impressive. In fact, the whole thing was so thin she could hardly imagine how it had stood up to the onslaught of the soldiers for so long.

"It's made out of beds," Ib said.

"Beds?"

"Yeah. You know those things that fix your health? Ever seen one of them break?"

Brit realized she had not.

"Now, come on," Ib said impatiently, "let's go see gramps."

And with that, he skipped off into the dusk of the suburbs, Brit and the others hurrying to follow.

Chapter 12

Brit was surprised by how little the suburbs had changed since her last visit. The barricade was new, and there was a distinct lack of classed NPCs, but besides that the suburbs remained unchanged.

The streets were still gloomy. The sun was hidden away behind Zenith City, leaving only lamplight to illuminate the suburbs. And the lamps gave off dingy, almost fluorescent light. A yellowing light that cast all flesh as sickly.

The buildings of the suburbs grew organically in a hodgepodge of heights and angles. Some blocks were neat townhouses, built like a gated community. But most of the buildings had sprung up like wings.

They cannibalized each other's airspace, leaned against each other for support and in some cases even forced each other out. Many windows were boarded up. Brit couldn't tell if that was done due to vacancy or as a rudimentary defense.

She also noticed that they were casting a wide arc away from the columns. The basic roadmap of the suburbs was a grid, albeit a skewed grid. Yet, instead of walking the minimum distance, they took side streets. Streets where the houses leaned forward like they were praying, touching over the center to form tunnels for pedestrians.

The Citizens they passed stared openly at the party. Brit received nothing but looks of suspicion. But Ib's presence did wonders. Even if a Citizen twitched for their weapon, one look at the boy calmed whatever fears they had.

As for Ib, he talked a mile a minute the whole way. Brit tried to keep up as he told her how Hawthorne led the Citizens against the soldiers and took charge of the barricade. He spoke so quickly Brit only managed to inject the stray "Yeah" or "Uh-huh" into his torrent of words.

Finally, he stopped to catch his breath. Seizing the opportunity, Brit asked, "Did anyone change?"

Ib answered her slowly. "I got better at fighting," he said. "I'm real good now, honest."

"No, I mean, did anyone . . . " Brit wasn't sure how to put it. *Is anyone a monster now? Did you have to put anyone down?* She wondered how believable her story would be if none of the Zenith Citizens were transmogrified.

"Has anyone here become monsters?" Lynx asked. "They would have skin like stone and claws like blades."

"You must be joking," one of the adults said. "People don't just change into monsters."

Leo choked out a laugh. "You have no idea. Consider yourself fortunate."

It was impossible to judge time in the suburbs, but Brit guessed they had been walking for half an hour. The artificial twilight left her completely unmoored and disoriented. Another left turn and they were there. Brit remembered the street, the particular backwards lean of its buildings.

None of the windows were boarded up on this street. Through them Brit saw families. Fathers sat at tables with sons, eating small meals. Or in cleared-away rooms, mothers practiced warcraft with their daughters. Even the lamplight seemed brighter, lighter on this boulevard.

Hawthorne was sitting on his stoop, conversing with Mikayla and his granddaughter Henny. Brit wasn't surprised to see Henny had grown up as much as Ib. As the party approached, he rose on wobbly legs, leaning heavily on his stick. He looked just the same as ever—an ornery old coot. Henny gripped his arm to steady him, but he pulled it away and limped toward Brit.

"Took your time coming back, didn't you? Could've used you and your gang a month ago."

Brit couldn't help smiling. "It's good to see you too, you old coot."

He leaned close and whispered, "I'm sorry to hear about Suzanne. We'll get them."

Brit was too surprised to reply. Mikayla caught her eye and nodded—she must have told Hawthorne the whole story.

"Some of you I recognize," Hawthorne said, nodding to Burgrave and Crux, "and some of you, I don't. But you're welcome in my home as long as Mikayla says you're okay. And she says you're okay. So come on in."

Not waiting for courtesy, he hobbled up the stairs and into his home. It was furnished with meager furniture. The party was too large to all fit around Hawthorne's table, so it was pushed back against a wall. More chairs were produced and set up in a circle. Hawthorne sat by the door, with Mikayla on his left. Brit sat next to Mikayla, with Burgrave and Crux on her left; then Lynx, Leo, Mallon, and Ib, who completed the circle at Hawthorn's right.

Once they were all seated, Hawthorne said, "A few introductions are in order."

"I think you know Burgrave and Crux," Brit said.

"By reputation if nothing else," Hawthorne agreed.

"Likewise, your reputation precedes you," Burgrave said.

"All good I hope. And who are you two?"

"May I present Princess Lynx and Prince Leo of Pyxis, and Mallon, also of Pyxis."

"Royalty!" Hawthorne exclaimed. "Apologies for the accommodations. Wasn't expecting to see nobles around here."

Lynx offered a glassy smile. "You have done more than enough. Thank you for welcoming us to your home."

"Alright then," Hawthorne continued, "Mikayla was just about to tell me what brings you to our fair suburb."

"We're going up to Zenith City," Mikayla said.

"What's in Zenith City?" Hawthorne asked.

The party exchanged looks. "Xenos," Brit growled.

"What's a Xenos?" Ib asked.

Burgrave shushed him, then repeated the question.

"A monster in the guise of a man," Leo muttered.

"Plenty of those going around," Hawthorne replied. "Anything else I might know him by?"

How could Brit explain Xenos? She didn't know that much about the NPC herself. "He wears a long robe. It's purple. And, uh, he has a hood, so you can't really see his face. And he's usually surrounded by really tough fighters. And when you're around him you feel kind of, um, weird," she finished, knowing how lame her description sounded.

"He is not very nice," Crux added.

"Got it. So you're looking for a not-nice man in a hood."

"He is an ally of Ramses," Burgrave added.

"Beg pardon," Hawthorne responded, "but weren't you?"

A bark of laughter slipped out of Brit.

Mikayla stood up. "He's doing something to Citizens," she said. "He's making them into monsters. None of us know how he does it. I haven't seen it here, but it's been happening everywhere else."

"Everywhere?" Hawthorne asked.

"We've been all over Pyxis and Altair," Brit answered.

Mikayla continued. "They look like they're made out of stone. Big claws, spines on their arms and shoulders. Have you seen any Citizens like that?"

Hawthorne shook his head. "Can't say that I have."

"Well, there's an army of them marching up the Grand Highway," Mikayla said. "We got ahead of them, but I don't know how big our lead is."

Hawthorne stroked his chin, thinking. "You say this Xenos wears a purple robe?"

"Yes. I've never seen anyone else quite like him," Mallon replied. "And I've seen a lot."

"And he's up in the city?"

Brit realized the party was looking at her. "I think so," she said. "It feels like that's where he is."

"Soon as that monster army gets here, we'll have our hands full holding the walls. Assuming we can hold them. But we'll give you enough time to do what you've got to do."

He turned to Ib. "Go tell the others to gather by the western barricade. You tell them I said they've got to come. I said it was time."

Ib nodded and rose. He was at the door when Hawthorne added, "Tell 'em to come armed or not to come at all."

Ib paused for a second.

"Get," Hawthorne commanded, and Ib got.

No one said anything until the door shut.

"Hawthorne, thank you," Lynx said.

Hawthorne waved his hand dismissively. "You got to promise me something. You got to promise that you'll deal with this Xenos. It doesn't matter if you come back. Figure I won't be around to yell at you if you whiff. Don't whiff. Get him. Promise me."

"I promise," Brit said. "We'll bring the whole fucking city down if we have to. But we're going to get him. I swear it."

"Good," Hawthorne said. A twisted smile spread over his face. It wasn't a happy expression, but it was content all the same.

An hour later, Brit stood with Hawthorne and the rest of the party on the stoop of Hawthorne's home. More than a hundred NPCs were assembled in the street before them—all Citizens. The crowd bristled with makeshift weaponry and slapdash armor.

They weren't an army, Brit knew that much. She had fought with and against armies before. These Citizens made nervous chatter among themselves, shuffling into clusters. Not a single item was standard among their ranks.

Ib had a table leg sharpened to a point on one end. An iron ball was affixed to the other end. He tapped the ball against his palm, shifting his weight from leg to leg. He wore two sheets of metal, like a sandwich board, draped over his torso. A crock-pot was his helmet. That comprised the sum of his armor.

Brit scanned the crowd of Zenith Citizens. Ib was the best equipped of any of them.

"Are they going to prepare themselves?" Lynx asked. Brit fought the urge to kick her.

"Oh, they're prepared all right," Hawthorne said grimly. "This is the elite."

He chuckled humorlessly.

"Like I said, we'll clear the way. Can't say for how long."

"It will be enough," Burgrave said. He looked as calm as ever.

"How can you know?" Lynx asked, her voice sharp with anxiety. Brit was also curious where the diminutive NPC's confidence came from.

"Either our forces will be sufficient or they will not," Burgrave answered steadily. "At this point, we can do little to change that. So I choose to remain positive."

"I never figured you for an optimist, Burgy," Brit said.

"I draw breath," Burgrave said. "Of course, I believe it will all work out."

And he smiled. Brit had never seen him smile

before. Up until that moment, she half-believed that smiling wasn't in his programming.

Mikayla walked up to them. "We should say something to them. I've been walking around down there and they're nervous."

"No shit," Brit laughed.

"They'd be odd ducks if they weren't nervous," Mallon added.

"Yeah, but we don't want them backing out now," Mikayla said. "I heard some of them talking about ditching."

"As soon as one goes, others will follow," Leo said. He turned to Hawthorne. "I thought you said they were prepared."

"Don't get your royalty in a bunch," Hawthorne replied. "I said they were ready, and they're as ready as they're going to get. They aren't soldiers. They defended their homes and that's it. Now you're asking them to fight, and that's fine, that's good, but they haven't fought like this before. All they've got is rumors of the enemy, and that makes them jumpy."

Out of nowhere came a huge crashing noise, weapon against armor. The whole party jumped. Brit looked around for the noise.

Crux stood in front of the stoop, holding his old armor, the suit he wore as captain of the Zenith City Guard with one hand and his massive war hammer with the other.

"What the hell is he doing?" Mikayla asked.

"Hey Crux," Brit called, but Crux ignored her. He raised his hammer high and smashed it once more into the armor. Everyone jumped again and the crowd of Citizens was quiet.

"Friends," Crux boomed. "I do not know what else to call you but friends. I want you all to follow me. We are going to save the world and we need your help."

"No, you don't," one of the Citizens shouted. "You just need us as sacrifice. You'll stick to the back and let those creatures gobble us up while you make a break for it." Brit searched the crowd for the heckler but couldn't discern who it was.

Whoever they were, their comments didn't seem to faze Crux at all. He took a step forward into the crowd.

"Look at me," the giant bellowed. "Do I look like I stay at the back? Do I look like I make a break for it?"

No one dared heckle him, although that might have partially been due to the fact that the tallest Citizen came up to his elbows.

"Follow me!" He waded through the crowd. Citizens stepped to the side to accommodate him. Once he was at the other side, he turned back. Besides getting out of his way, none of the Citizens had moved.

Crux lifted his hammer and smashed the head into the ground, cracking the road, launching rubble in every direction. "Follow me!" he shouted, and they did. Galvanized into action, the Citizens half-stumbled into a loose formation behind him, leaving Brit and the others on the stoop.

"I never heard him say so many words before," Mallon mused.

"What're you waiting for?" Hawthorne asked. "You got to get up there!"

Brit looked around at the party. Burgrave was staring off after Crux and the receding crowds, his scimitar stuck through his belt. Lynx and Leo both held their weapons in their hands, the heads of their naginata and stave almost touching. Only Mallon looked truly relaxed with her whip coiled around her body.

And then there was Mikayla.

She looked tired. Maybe it was the shadows of the suburbs, but she looked like a strong breeze would knock her over. Yet even as Brit thought that, Mikayla raised her head and met Brit's gaze. She smiled and Brit felt a warmth spread through her. Not confidence, but as Burgrave had said, acceptance. The only way forward was forward.

The party marched toward the southeastern pillar of Zenith City, which held an elevator up to the city. A panel slid open, admitting the six of them. As the door slid shut behind them, Mikayla grabbed onto Brit's hand. Brit gave her hand a squeeze.

"Okay," Brit said. "Let's go cause a ruckus."

Chapter 13

Suzanne woke up.

No, she didn't. She had been awake, had felt Gemini's knife go into her body. It hadn't hurt. She watched her health bar drop to nothing with a mixture of curiosity and calm fear. Almost like she was lying on the shore and letting the tide slowly drown her.

Her hand pixelated first. She heard Mikayla shout her name and said something back, but it was inconsequential. Then her torso went and she was dead. It all happened in a couple of seconds. Long seconds while she was pixelating. Though now they seemed as short as any other.

And now she was—where was she? She looked down and did not see anything beneath her. No floor, but more disconcerting, no body. Yet, Suzanne could still feel herself, her limits. She curled a hand into a fist and felt the slight touch of fingers on a palm. But there was no palm and no fingers.

Was she dead? Was this what death felt like? To Suzanne, death was a coffin lowering into a grave—her mother's coffin. She didn't feel entombed or claustrophobic at all. In fact, the space around her felt infinite.

She closed her eyes. Nothing changed, she was still in the void. But she tried to remember what it had felt like. Her body dislocated, spread out into pixels. She could almost remember one instant of it, when she had lost form completely. She felt the wind blow through her, completely enveloping her. Every bit of her touched the breeze. Her skin did not touch skin or her insides, but breeze on all sides. She shivered, remembering how that felt.

Suzanne opened her eyes. Off in the distance was a single pixel of light.

"Log out," Suzanne said to the pixel. The words echoed from all around her.

Nothing happened.

"New game," Suzanne said.

Nothing happened.

"Fuck you," Suzanne said.

Nothing happened as a result of that either. Suzanne tried taking a step. Toes, five on each foot, felt the ground beneath her. Nothing was there, but as she took a step she felt pressure meeting her, equaling her weight. She took another step and more floor rose up beneath her.

She walked into the void. It was constant darkness save the one pixel. Suzanne kept walking. The pixel did not grow any larger, but she did not turn back. How long she walked for she did not know. She lost track of time, or was it that time had lost interest in her? Surely, it was an hour, a month. Surely, the sun had collapsed and swallowed the solar system by now. And still there was just the pixel off in the distance.

Until there was not. There was a light. Several lights, spelling out the words, SELECT A SAVE FILE.

"Okay," Suzanne said.

The lights bled away from her, receding and reassembling into shapes.

The first shape was her. She recognized her nose first and worked out the rest from her nose.

CLASS: INFILTRATOR, the lights read. NAME: SUZANNE. Her stats were listed beneath her name. Small graphics represented each of the items that had been in her inventory.

"That one," Suzanne said, pointing with her hand that was not there.

The lights reassembled into a shroud around the character. It thickened until it was opaque and then receded, leaving a silhouette where Suzanne had been.

CANNOT SELECT. CHARACTER DEAD.

"Okay," Suzanne said. "Fine."

Next to the silhouette was Brit. Her face was furious. Whatever she was up to was clearly pissing her off.

The lights hurried over to Brit and began to spell again. CLASS: DRAGOON, they read. NAME: BRIT.

"That one," Suzanne said. She figured it wouldn't work and didn't really want it to.

CANNOT SELECT. CHARACTER IN USE.

"At least she's still alive," Suzanne said. The lights did not respond to her comment.

The next character was Mikayla. She looked frustrated. Not as much as Brit, but clearly annoyed all the same.

CLASS: SWIFTBLADE. NAME: MIKAYLA. CANNOT SELECT. CHARACTER IN USE.

"Okay," Suzanne said. "Fine. Thank you for letting me know."

They were okay. Or at least alive. That was something to be thankful for.

It was then that Suzanne saw the fourth shape. She looked at it and it came into focus. The lights moved over to it and began to spell.

CLASS: ASSASSIN, they read.

With the lights above it, Suzanne could see that it

was Gemini. Her face was perfectly still. Like Gemini was asleep.

NAME: SUZANNE, the lights read.

"Suzanne?" Suzanne said.

Gemini's—no, Suzanne's—stats trailed below. Suzanne looked them over and felt like the biggest idiot ever.

She recognized the stat spread. It should have been obvious from the first time she saw Gemini without her mask. How could she have missed it?

Gemini was her first player character.

Before she had let Brit and Mikayla try the game. When Io was still only on a screen, Suzanne had played the game alone. Solo beta testing. As soon as Brit and Mikayla became adequate players, as soon as they had all acclimated to the TII, Suzanne had made a new character so they would all be at the same level.

That was why Gemini looked like her. That was why Gemini was so powerful. Suzanne had ground through the game, testing every aspect of combat. And however Gemini had come to be animate on her own, maybe that explained why she hated Suzanne. Because Suzanne had abandoned her.

Well, now Suzanne was taking her back.

"That's the one," she said to the lights.

They faded and reappeared. ENJOY THE GAME.

"I will," Suzanne said, as Io rushed into being all around her and she fell and she fell and she fell into a body.

Suzanne woke up. In a field, this time. The grass tickled her face. She saw she was wearing a long black cloak and leather gloves, like Gemini's. *So it wasn't just a dream*, Suzanne thought. *I guess I'm Gemini now.*

She sat up and looked around, ducking as something small flew by her head.

The creature's tiny wings beat so quickly they looked like a blue blur. It took Suzanne a moment to realize it was a faerie. But the only faeries in Io were in the Meadow of Beginnings. Is that where she was?

Suzanne stood up and looked around. Sure enough, the Meadow extended to the horizon in every direction. She ran her hands over the blades of grass, enjoying the pleasure of touching again.

Up ahead, the grass rustled. Whatever was in there was far too large to be a faerie. Suzanne saw the red diamond icon twirling over the creature's head and reached for the daggers on her belt.

But that wasn't where Gemini kept her daggers—a fact Suzanne realized as the goblin sprang out of the grass and thrust its spear at her. Suzanne raised her arms to protect herself and the spear broke against the leather gauntlets around her wrist.

The goblin—which was the size of a child, with sickly white skin—looked from the pixelating shaft of his broken spear up to the Assassin towering over him.

Suzanne laughed. She had forgotten how weak the enemies were in the tutorial level. They were hardly a challenge for level one players. They couldn't even scratch someone as high-leveled as the Assassin avatar.

Suzanne punted the goblin off into the Meadow. Somewhere in the clouds he popped into pixels and dispersed.

Now to find Igor. Igor Redcap was the goblin boss of the Meadow, and once Suzanne beat him she could get back into Io proper.

Suzanne dug through her inventory, looking for a weapon. Even if Igor was as weak as she remembered, she didn't want to take any chances. Seeing as she had so recently been reincarnated, she wasn't trying to die again.

Next to a couple of smoke bombs, Suzanne found a pair of curved daggers that she'd felt the blade of too many times. But they would do. And next to them, she saw with a thrill of triumph, was the gold and green key to the Oracle Chamber.

When she found Igor Redcap minutes later, Suzanne didn't even wait for him to finish his speech. She cut his arm off before he could draw his sword and dispatched with the goblin chief before he could cry out in pain. As his body pixelated, a door appeared.

Finally! Suzanne flung the door wide open and stepped through, returning to Io.

Suzanne found herself at the end of the Grand Highway. But she wasn't alone. As far as she could see were transformed Citizens, like a huge stone snake winding its way up the highway.

Suzanne froze. But the creatures had already noticed her. One of them turned around and glared at her with yellow eyes.

So much for an extra life, Suzanne thought, drawing her daggers. But the creature merely stared at her before continuing forward.

Maybe they think I'm Gemini. If that was the case, then she could follow them up the road to Zenith City without a problem. The fastest way there was going on the highway, after all. Seeing no better options,

Suzanne followed the tail of the column through the day into the night and the next.

Zenith City was visible for miles as she walked up the Grand Highway, but the suburbs only came into view as she drew closer. And someone had set up a barricade in between the buildings of Zenith City. It was nearly two stories high. The barricade hadn't stopped the creatures though. They had smashed straight through, leaving a hole twice as wide as Suzanne was tall.

She could hear the sounds of a battle inside the city. Whoever was fighting against the creatures couldn't be doing well.

Suzanne broke off from the creatures, walking west around the city until she could no longer hear them fighting. Once they were out of earshot, she drew her daggers. Stabbing them into the wall she began to climb. In a matter of minutes, she was up and over the barricade and into the gloom of the suburbs.

The streets of the suburbs were deserted as well. The solitude was oppressive. But she could hear faint sounds of conflict emanating from one of the other pillars. Suzanne skirted around a massive pothole in the road, making toward the sound of violence. She had no doubt that if there was a fight, Brit and Mikayla couldn't be too far.

She did not see Brit or Mikayla. All she saw were row after row of transmogrified Citizens, huddled around Crux.

Crux had backed himself up against a wall. He swung his hammer in a semicircle, keeping the creatures at bay. There were hundreds of them, more coming in from all sides. She couldn't hear the crunch of his hammer hitting the ones that got too close over the sound of their collective hissing.

"Crux!" She cupped her hands around her mouth, shouting. He glanced up and saw her and his face hardened. Suzanne remembered she looked like Gemini. And Gemini had killed Suzanne. And Suzanne was Crux's friend.

She could see the gears turning in Crux's head. He leapt forward, his hammer's head glowed and he slammed it into the ground. The pavement cracked under impact, fissures spider-webbing out in every direction. The ground rose in a wave, crashing out in all directions. It knocked the creatures off their feet.

Suzanne leapt over the wave of earth as it rolled past, landing on one side. Crux was charging toward her. The Monk and the Berserker had been easy enough, but she couldn't fight Crux. She needed him.

"Wait!" she shouted. "It's me! It's Suzanne!"

But Crux didn't wait. He charged straight at her and she barely threw herself to the side in time. Suzanne racked her memory, trying to think of something that would prove her identity to the giant.

"You rescued me from Fenhold!" she said, ducking under a hammer stroke that would have taken off her head.

"We found Burgrave in Glensia together!" she yelled, but that didn't work either. By now, the creatures were clambering back up onto their feet. She couldn't dodge Crux and the creatures. She had to take this somewhere else.

She saw the column behind Crux. A desperate idea hit her. The next time he charged her she ran straight at him. She leapt, vaulting over his shoulders and hit the ground running. Crux turned and chased after her, bludgeoning any Citizen that got in his way into the next block.

Suzanne reached the column and slammed her hands against its base. The elevator door slid open and the green light flicked on. Crux smashed through the door as it tried to close. With a stutter, the door slammed shut.

Now it was just her and him. Of course, that didn't necessarily make her any safer.

"You've got to believe me!" she yelled, ducking as he slammed his hammer at her. His blow struck the side of the elevator, shaking the compartment.

Suzanne realized Crux wasn't going to listen to her. She had to fight back. Using her elbows, her knees, her fists—but not her blades—to beat him down. She ducked his attacks, went under him, and over him. She bounced off the walls and let him tire himself out.

Finally, he let the massive hammer fall from his grip.

"Kill me," he said. His simple face was not angry but unfathomably sad. "I cannot avenge her. Kill me like you killed her."

Something about his submission enraged Suzanne. "I told you I was Suzanne, you dick!" she shouted, kicking him in the knee. He hardly registered her blow.

"Why won't you believe me? You saved me, remember? All those nights we talked when I was in the dungeon? And you would say, every single time, 'Will I see you tomorrow?' Like I had a choice!"

A glimmer of recognition appeared in Crux's eyes.

"Remember when we found Burgrave? And you were so happy? What if Burgrave hadn't believed that you were on his side? That's how this feels."

The elevator continued its climb toward Zenith City. High above, Suzanne could see stars dotting the night sky.

"Suzanne?" Crux still sounded skeptical.

"Come on!" she said. "What else do I have to do to prove that it's me?"

"How could it be you?"

Suzanne hadn't expected that question. She had no idea how to explain save files and character selection to Crux. "I don't know," she said. "But it's me."

Crux answered by surging forward and wrapping her in a bear hug. "I do not know how this happened," he rumbled, "but I am very glad you are you."

Chapter 14

The elevator slowed as they reached street level. It rose right through the cobblestones, the platform filling the empty area of the column. Brit stepped off the platform. The rest of the party followed, their footsteps loud in the quiet city. Brit blinked the glare away from her eyes, searching the square for any signs of life.

The pillar they rode up let them out into the market square. Rows of merchant stalls extended in each direction, filling the square. But this being Zenith City, the stalls were far from average. Each was colorfully decorated in whichever way its merchant thought would be most eye-catching. Some were gilded, some shown with the entire spectrum of the rainbow. Armorers had hung their best pieces, polished to a glow, front and center. Most of the weapon-smiths opted to display their range. Spears hung by arrows, swords butted into cudgels. Brit's gaze lingered on an array of bejeweled halberds that were as beautiful as they were useless.

At the perimeter of the square sat inns and other permanent edifices. Peeking over the top of those buildings Brit saw the coliseum's round, open roof. In the opposite direction was the imperious Zenith Castle.

All were empty.

The party moved toward the castle, passing through the rows of stalls. At each row they stopped and checked and at each row they were met with nothing. Brit kicked a loose cobblestone. It skittered over the ground—the only other moving thing in the Capital.

"We ought to re-equip," Leo said, eyeing a display of spears.

Brit laughed. "It's all junk. You'd be better off fighting with their brooms."

She remembered the last time she had haggled with a merchant in Zenith City. Brit had been able to bend one of his spear-points between two of her fingers. She still had to pay for the ruined merchandise, but the look on his face had been worth the hefty price tag.

Mallon sighed and shook her head. "Biggest damn city in the world and you're telling me all their gear is bunk?"

"Not all the gear," Brit replied. "Just all the shit the merchants sell. The armory for Ramses's army was good enough."

"An armory which is now empty, I am afraid," Burgrave said.

"We should at least rest," he added. "We do not know what awaits us at the castle."

Brit glanced at her health bar. She still had about eighty percent left, but there was sense in what Burgrave was saying.

"What about the Citizens?" Lynx said. "What about Crux? We cannot dawdle! We must end this now."

No one spoke. Brit guessed they were all thinking

what she was, but none of them wanted to say it. To her surprise, it was Mikayla who finally spoke up.

"We won't be able to save them," she said. "They made their choice. And Crux, too—he knew what was going on. All we can do now is make sure we end this."

Lynx glared at Mikayla, but Brit knew there was no anger there. Just the shared disappointment of the party.

"If there are no further objections then I suggest we rest," Burgrave said. There were none. He led the way to the edge of the square, to an inn called the Weremonkey's Paw. He knocked twice before opening the door.

The Weremonkey's Paw was unspectacular on the inside. The unquenchable fire burning in the fireplace was the only light. Opposite the door was a counter doubling as a bar. Two staircases flanked the counter, leading up to the second level with the beds.

"Two hours," Mikayla said. "Everybody cool with that?"

When no one said otherwise she headed off toward

the steps. Brit followed her up the stairs and into a room, closing the door behind her.

Brit unequipped her armor.

"Put it back on," Mikayla said, her voice hard.

Brit looked at her, confused.

"We don't have time for *that*. And what if something attacks us?"

"Like what?"

"Like anything! I just . . . I just keep thinking something's going to jump out at us. I mean do you really think we're just going to walk up to the castle? Don't you think Xenos has some kind of welcoming party? We're behind enemy lines. We can't relax."

Brit laughed. Mikayla was right, of course, but she sounded ridiculous.

"What?" Mikayla demanded.

"Nothing," Brit said, trying her best to sound earnest despite the giggles escaping her. "You're right, it's just funny hearing you sound so . . . militaristic."

"Hey, SAT word," Mikayla said. Her expression

softened. "Keep your eyes on the prize. We're fighting for our lives and the right to be bored in history class."

They laughed. "Through great sacrifice we have achieved our goal of going back to high school," Brit intoned with great solemnity.

"The Quest for Study Hall, no, The Fellowship of Free Period!" Mikayla said.

They laughed until they were done laughing. Brit's thoughts turned to Suzanne. She didn't ignore them and they sobered her.

"Let's get some rest," Mikayla said. From the way she was looking at Brit—like she was fragile, the most precious thing in the universe—Brit knew Mikayla's thoughts had gone to Suzanne, too.

"I only need twenty minutes," Brit said. "Wake me up then." She leaned back into the pillow and let Io put her to sleep with a smile still on her face.

Mikayla shook her awake twenty minutes later.

Mikayla dropped off to sleep. Brit passed the time watching her, watching the way her mouth barely moved as her sleeping body inhaled and exhaled, staying alive. Mikayla had said to wake her up after an hour, but Brit let her sleep longer, waking her up just a few minutes before it was time for the party to reassemble.

They met back up in the common room of the Weremonkey's Paw. No one looked particularly well rested. Brit was feeling jumpy herself.

"Shall we?" Lynx said.

"Let's go fuck him up," Brit replied.

They trailed out of the inn, following the empty streets to Zenith Castle. The emptiness was beginning to get to Brit. The echoes were getting under her skin. She kept waiting for something—a gargoyle, a soldier, anything—to jump out at them, but nothing did. Contrary to what Mikayla had said, it appeared Xenos did not have a welcoming party waiting for them. Nothing happened except them walking until they reached the castle.

And the castle? It was just as Brit remembered leaving it, draped with banners showing Ramses's sigil. It was splendid, Brit supposed, if you went in for castles. The huge double doors, split down the middle, were shut.

Brit knocked. No response.

"Anyone have the key?" she asked.

No response.

"Anyone good at picking locks?"

No response.

"Alright then," Brit said. She took a few steps back, then charged forward, slamming her halberd into the door.

It bounced with a dull thunk.

"Shit," she said. She took another swing at it, and the door responded with the same thunk.

"Okay," she said. "Time to get serious."

She backed away from the door, all the way across the road. Motioning to the others to get out of her way, she fired up another Bull Rush. She didn't bother swinging her halberd this time.

Brit slammed into the door and bounced off. The Bull Rush shot her forward again and she slammed into the door again and bounced off, again. This kept up until the Bull Rush timed out.

"What the fuck!" Brit shouted, slamming her fist into the door. All this earned her was yet another thunk. Brit started pummeling the door, throwing punches as hard as she could.

Thunk, thunk, thunk.

"Brit," Mikayla said, grabbing Brit's arm. Brit felt her grip but wasn't able to check herself in time. Her strength pulled Mikayla forward, sending her stumbling into the door.

Thunk.

"Are you okay?" Brit said.

"I'm fine," Mikayla said, dusting herself off. "But you need to calm down."

The rest of the party tried, one by one. Brit sank to sitting as they took their best shots and bounced off.

"Is this it?" she asked no one in particular. "After

every fucking thing we got through, a door stops us? Really?"

No one answered her. There was no answer, just the echoed thunks and the wind whispering over the empty city like laughter.

Thunk, thunk, thunk.

"What is that?" Suzanne said. The sound had been growing louder as they approached Zenith Castle. The sun was completely gone from the sky. Street lamps turned on, illuminating the city as soon as night fell.

The city was empty, but despite that Suzanne could have sworn someone was watching her. She kept glancing back over her shoulder. No one was there and there was no sound beside the increasingly loud thunks.

"I know not what they be," Crux replied.

Suzanne had meant her question rhetorically. Crux was so quiet, despite his size, that she started at the sound of his voice.

"I guess we'll find out soon enough," she said.

And they did. As they turned the corner onto the street where Zenith Castle was, Suzanne saw what was causing the ruckus.

On the other side of the castle's drawbridge, the rest of her party was assembled. Mallon, Lynx, and Burgrave were sitting on the side of the bridge, their heads bent in conversation. Suzanne was shocked to see Leo with them. Brit and Mikayla had said he was working for Xenos, but maybe the prince had come to his senses.

Mikayla stood closer to the door, her arms spread wide, clearly trying to reason with Brit.

And Brit? She was the one thunking, punching the door again and again to no effect.

"Friends!" Crux shouted.

Thunk. The party all stared at him.

"You made it!" Lynx shouted. She took a step forward, but Leo grabbed her arm.

"Wait," he said. "Who is that with you?"

"It's me!" Suzanne yelled. She realized how idiotic

that sounded and was about to explain more, but by then Brit had already charged. Suzanne was always surprised by how fast Brit was, every time she saw her move. Dragoons were built to be tanks. She should know, having designed the classes herself.

Brit was a foot away when Suzanne realized she needed to move like yesterday. She threw herself backwards but stumbled over Gemini's cloak and found herself sitting on her ass with a very large halberd and a very pissed Dragoon staring her down.

"Is that really the best you can do, bitch?" Brit asked. "Get the fuck up."

"Brit," Suzanne said. "It's me."

"I know that," Brit said. Her voice was calm, too calm. Her eyes were livid.

"I'm Suzanne," she said. "I'm—"

The rest of her sentence was knocked out of her mouth as Brit slapped the flat of her halberd across Suzanne's face.

"Don't," Brit said. "Don't. Say. Her. Name."

"But it is Suzanne!" Crux said. *About fucking time he said something,* Suzanne thought.

"Bullshit," Brit said.

By now the rest of the party had arrived, their weapons drawn.

"Move away from her, Crux," Burgrave said.

"Burgrave—" Crux started, but a glare from Burgrave silenced him.

"You have been deceived," Burgrave said. "Or if you have not been deceived you have been turned. Either way, step away from her."

Crux looked at each of the party members in turn, finally turning to look down on Suzanne.

He took a step to the side. "She is Suzanne," he muttered in a tone like a chastised child. Another withering look from Burgrave silenced him.

"What do we do with her?" Mallon asked. Suzanne had never seen the old Pyxian look angry before, but she looked positively bloodthirsty.

"We end her," Leo said. There was nothing but

contempt in his voice. Clearly someone had told him how Suzanne's previous avatar had died.

"Good thinking," Brit said, raising her halberd.

"No!" Suzanne shouted. "It's me!" She would have said more, but Mallon's whip lashed out, wrapping around her throat. Suzanne pulled against the whip, but it was wrapped tight, effectively gagging her.

Brit swung her halberd down. Suzanne closed her eyes.

There was a loud clang. Suzanne's eyes snapped open and she saw Mikayla had caught the halberd between her two crossed swords.

"What the fuck are you doing?" Brit yelled.

"No," Mikayla said. "We need her." She turned Brit's halberd and drove it into the ground.

"Let her go," Mikayla said to Mallon. Mallon frowned but didn't argue, letting her whip go back.

"Now you," Mikayla said to Suzanne. "Get up."

Suzanne got up. "Thanks," she said.

"Don't talk to me," Mikayla spat back at her.

"We're going to walk toward that door, okay? And you're going to pick the lock. You try anything and I won't stop Brit next time. Now move."

She prodded Suzanne with the flat of her blade.

Suzanne stumbled forward under the baleful gazes of her party, the people and NPCs she trusted most in the world. She racked her brain, trying to come up with some way to convince them that she was who she said she was. Maybe if she unlocked the door they would believe her.

She stooped by the door and initiated the lock-picking mini-game. It took the form of a sliding block puzzle, an easy one at that. When the puzzle was complete, the lock clicked open.

"Now listen," Suzanne began, standing up, but Mikayla stabbed at her chest and she threw herself sideways out of range. Brit was there, grabbing her arms and pinning them behind her back.

"Do it," Brit said. Suzanne struggled as hard as she could but couldn't break free of Brit's grip. Mikayla advanced, scraping her sword over the pavement.

"I'd ask if you have any last words," Mikayla said, "but they'd probably be lies."

And then the perfect words occurred to Suzanne.

"You were right," she said. "I'm talking to you, Brit. It would be way better dying in Io than living in New Jersey."

Mikayla stopped. "What did you say?"

"It's just that, if my dad's gonna move us anyway, then I might as well die here. I mean, how would I make it through high school without my two best friends?"

"What is she talking about?" Lynx asked. Suzanne ignored her. She was staring straight at Mikayla, willing Mikayla to believe the words she was saying.

"For all I know Jersey will be full of Gretchens," Suzanne said. "I won't be friends with anyone on the cheerleading team who can tell her to fuck off."

"Oh my god," Mikayla said. Her sword slipped from her hands and clattered on the ground.

"And Brit," Suzanne said, "who's going to pull the

fire alarm when I need to get out of class? Who's going to get me outside of detention?"

Suzanne heard Brit's sharp intake of air and felt Brit's grip slacken just enough to pull herself free. She jumped toward the door, away from Brit grabbing after her and put her hands up in the air.

"My name is Suzanne Thurston," she said. "I'm a junior at Perry Hall High School. My mom died when I was thirteen years old. I hate the way eggs taste and I'm nearsighted. What else can I tell you two to make you believe me?"

"Oh my god," Mikayla said. "Is it really you?"

"Our Intro to Tech teacher is named Mr. Wells," Suzanne said. "Our history teacher is named—"

She couldn't finish the sentence as Brit and Mikayla leapt on her and embraced her in a hug tighter than Crux's had been.

"How the fuck did this happen?" Brit was shouting. Mikayla was making weird sounds that were half-shouted laughter and half-sob.

Suzanne managed to gasp, "Let me down and I'll

tell you!" When they finally let her down, she explained what had happened as best she could without explicitly mentioning a log-in screen. There were still NPCs around so Suzanne had to watch what she said. After she was finished, Burgrave walked over.

"If they believe you, so must I," he said. His tone was neutral. "I apologize for doubting you." Then a smile cracked across his face. "I am happy you have returned. The door was giving us considerable trouble."

Mallon embraced her in a quick hug, as did Lynx. Crux simply reminded everyone that he had been right.

Leo stared at her as if she wasn't real. "I didn't know," he said. "I should have known. There is nothing you cannot do."

"Thanks," she said. She hugged him. A friendly hug, and though he might have held on a little longer than she did, he still let go.

"Where were you going?" Suzanne asked, once everyone had calmed down.

"We were gonna go kill Xenos," Brit said. "You know, revenge and shit."

"But now we can go to the Oracle Chamber!" Mikayla said. "We can log out!"

A puzzled expression appeared on all of the NPCs faces. "That means we can go home," Suzanne hastily explained. That seemed to satisfy the NPCs, besides Burgrave, who remained suspicious.

Mallon cleared her throat and looked directly at Suzanne. "You once said the Oracle Chamber held the key to restoring our allies. To defeating these creatures."

"Yeah," Suzanne said.

"Then we will restore our allies and our kingdoms."

There was little room for argument from her tone. No one made one. The way forward was clear.

Chapter 15

The party headed into Zenith Castle. The last time Suzanne was in the castle was after Ramses fled south with his entire entourage. The castle was as empty now as it was then, but she couldn't shake the feeling that someone was still watching her through the long stone hallways.

Ramses had not been shy about how much he loved himself. Several ceiling-to-wall tapestries depicted the former king in various heroic poses. His sigil was everywhere. There was hardly a door, bench, wall, or chandelier that did not somehow represent the four pillars of the Altairi insignia.

"It's cold in here," Mikayla said. She shivered and rubbed her hands over her arms.

It was cold. Suzanne had only felt this cold once before in Io—in the crypt beneath Fenhold, Ramses's second castle. That was where she had seen Xenos reprogramming the king and where he had captured her. Io was supposed to be temperate at all times. The subterranean chill had been her first solid evidence that Xenos wasn't just another NPC.

"Are we ready?" Burgrave asked.

The party regarded each other. *Were they?* Suzanne had to wonder. Honestly, she had no idea what they were going up against. In every other fight, barring the ones against the transmogrified Citizens, she had at least a solid idea of what she was battling. She had written all the code herself and knew what each class was capable of, what each monster was weak against. The game was an open book to her.

But this was something way outside of what she could predict. Even if they ducked out and went to grind XP, trying to max out their characters before the final battle, it wouldn't matter if Xenos was operating outside the rules of the game. No matter how much they trained they would never really be ready, Suzanne realized.

"Fuck yeah," Brit said. "Born ready. Let's go get him."

"We will face him together," Lynx said. "He has much to pay for. Alphonse. The Citizens. Their spirits will be avenged."

"Well said," a cold voice replied. Xenos clapped softly as he emerged from the shadows of a hallway.

With a wordless roar, Leo charged at Xenos. The hooded NPC grabbed Leo by the collar and shoved him into the wall. Leo's head smacked into stone and the prince crumpled to the floor. Lynx cried out, but she didn't charge after her brother. *We have to fight him all at once or we won't stand a chance*, Suzanne thought.

Xenos kept walking as if nothing happened. "They are beautiful tapestries. This one in particular is my favorite," he said, gesturing to a large one which depicted an army of NPCs raising Zenith City's pillars.

"Even if the tapestry is a lie," Xenos continued. "You built these pillars, Suzanne. I'm surprised you would let anyone else take credit for them."

"What? How could Suzanne have built these when she is not even from Altair?" Mallon asked.

Xenos shrugged. "I suggest you ask her. But Suzanne is well used to others co-opting her creations. Like so."

He waved his hand and Leo's limp body shook. The NPCs eyes glowed white as he stood back up. The gray diamond over Leo's head turned red.

"After all we went through, Suzanne," Leo snarled. "How could you abandon me like that?"

He took a step toward her and smashed his stave into the floor. The stone tile shattered. Leo was strong, Suzanne knew, but he wasn't that strong.

"What are you doing?" Lynx asked. "Xenos is the enemy! Do not let him deceive you!"

"He doesn't really have a choice," Xenos chuckled. "And neither do you."

He waved his hand again and Lynx went limp. But the next moment her eyes glowed and she swung her naginata in a wide arc. Suzanne barely jumped out of the way in time. Brit shoved Lynx and she stumbled away from the rest of the party, toward Xenos and her brother.

"Now, who's next?" Xenos asked. Suzanne looked from Mallon, to Crux, to Burgrave, searching for which one would join Xenos's ranks next.

"I am sorry," Burgrave said. With a flash of his scimitar, he slashed through Crux's armor. Crux stared at Burgrave with fear in his eyes, but he couldn't raise his hammer against the Swiftblade.

I never saw him change, Suzanne thought. But then she realized Burgrave hadn't changed. Burgrave plunged his scimitar into Crux's stomach. Crux fell to his knees with a grunt as Burgrave turned his blade on himself.

"Avenge me," Burgrave said, cutting his own throat.

"Well, that was unexpected!" Xenos crowed. "But that still makes three on three." With another wave of his hand, Mallon uncoiled her whip and lashed at Suzanne's face. Suzanne jumped back and Brit threw her arm out. The whip coiled around her armor and Brit jerked on it, pulling Mallon off of her feet.

Lynx leapt forward, slashing with her naginata, but Mikayla checked her blow. The two of them stabbed and parried with such speed that Suzanne could barely follow their blades.

Which left her with Leo.

"I loved you!" he roared, swinging his stave at her head. Suzanne ducked as the stave tore a chunk out of the wall.

Suzanne drew her daggers. But before she could move, Leo was right in front of her, and he sent her stumbling with a savage punch.

You're an Assassin, Suzanne reminded herself. *You're faster now.* The next time Leo raised his stave she leapt forward and planted her daggers in his chest.

Leo staggered backwards. A look of horror spread over his face. "You already hurt me," he shouted. "Now it's my turn."

How is he still standing? Suzanne wondered. And then she realized—she was still in a party with Leo! That limited how much damage she could do to him. As he charged forward again she grabbed a smoke bomb and dropped it. The effect wouldn't last long, but it was enough time for her to navigate through her Menu. As she scrolled through the floating blue boxes, she found the icon for parties and cancelled out the ones she was in with Lynx, Leo, and Mallon. All of her other parties, besides the one she was in with Mikayla and Brit, had already been canceled out by the NPCs dying.

When the smoke cleared, she was ready. She threw a knife at Leo, who raised his stave to block. But in that moment Suzanne dove at his legs and slashed him below both knees. He fell, and before he could recover, Suzanne leapt on top of him and pinned him to the ground. She drove a dagger straight into his heart.

The wild look about his eyes relaxed. He looked like he did when she had first met him on the shores of the Ion River. He smiled as his body began to turn into pixels.

"Thank you," he said, and then he was gone.

Suzanne fell to the floor. She looked up and saw Brit hack through Mallon's silver whip. The old NPC struggled, but she was no match for Brit's muscles. With another swing of her halberd, Mallon joined Leo in pixelation.

Lynx's naginata clattered to the floor as Mikayla finished her off. The three friends looked at each other.

"I'm going to end him," Suzanne said softly. Neither Brit nor Mikayla had a response.

Xenos's chuckle floated down the hallways, and the girls followed it to the throne room.

Chapter 16

They arrived at a huge set of double doors. Each door was marked with a gem version of the sigil. Suzanne knew these were Energite. They put their hands on the sigils. With the sound of grinding gears, the doors swung open.

A soft laugh cut through the darkness like a knife.

"You finally made it." Xenos's disembodied voice filled Suzanne with a thrill of fear. "I was afraid you weren't coming."

"Laugh it up, fuckboy," Brit yelled back at him. After three steps forward the darkness enveloped her. Mikayla glanced back at Suzanne and smiled before stepping into the shadow after Brit. Suzanne took a deep breath and followed her friends forward into the abyss.

The door slammed shut behind her.

"I thought it might be more fun if it was just the four of us."

Suzanne couldn't see Xenos. She couldn't even see Brit and Suzanne. The throne room was pitch dark except for candelabras suspended from the ceiling high above. Their orange light didn't penetrate the darkness on the floor.

Suzanne banged her head into something hard.

"Brit?"

"Yeah."

"I'm gonna hold onto to you, okay?"

"Yeah."

Suzanne felt someone grab onto her cloak.

"It's me," Mikayla said.

They stumbled blindly forward for a few more steps. "This is bullshit," Brit muttered. "Hey Xenos! Turn on some fucking lights already! I want to see you when I'm beating the shit out of you."

Xenos's soft laugh echoed around the chamber. But then, to Suzanne's surprise, the room slowly brightened until she could clearly see.

Suzanne had forgotten how vast the chamber was. In her defense, she had never seen the throne room fully illuminated. Even when it housed Ramses, the king kept it dimly lit.

But in full light it was easily the size of a village. And all the way across the room, seated on Ramses's throne, was Xenos. He wore the same dark robe as always. It covered his arms and hands completely, its hood shrouding his features. But even at this distance Suzanne could clearly make out the sneer painted on his face.

"How did you like fighting those NPCs?"

His question hit Suzanne like a thunderbolt. How did Xenos know what an NPC was?

"Oh, come now, Suzanne. No need to look so surprised. You really thought you three kept your secret safe? I knew, of course. I always knew."

He rose from the throne and stepped forward. Not

down the stairs, but forward onto the air. There he floated, laughing.

"What are you?" Mikayla asked. Her hands were shaking so much that her swords were quivering.

"Suzanne knows," Xenos said. He floated down to the floor. "Or at least she should. After all, this is her world."

If Brit was curious about who Xenos was, she didn't show it. She charged forward, her halberd raised. But before she got within range of Xenos, he raised a hand. The tiled floor beneath Brit's feet turned into quicksand, sucking her down into the ground.

Brit flailed, but that only made the ground swallow her faster. Suzanne watched with horror as Brit was pulled in up to her waist, and then up to her shoulders. In another few seconds, her head would be under.

"Suzanne!" Mikayla shouted. Suzanne snapped out of her daze and rushed over. Together the two of them managed to pull Brit back out of the quicksand. There was a loud slurping noise as she finally came free.

Instantly, the quicksand turned back into tile.

Xenos laughed again. "It's insane, isn't it? The three of you are so vast, so powerful. And yet here you're nothing. Just insignificant specks."

A flame appeared in his hand. "I could end this right now, you know. It would be easy. I could end this for all of us."

He turned on the spot, vanishing and reappearing behind them. Before any of them could react, he lashed out, scattering them to the corners of the room with a series of pummeling blows.

Suzanne scrambled back onto her feet and glanced up at her health bar. Xenos had punched her twice and she only had a third of her health remaining.

He charged at her. No, *charging* implied he had to move. He flew at her. At the last minute, she threw herself aside, but Xenos stopped instantly.

"The trick with Gemini was nice," he said. "I can't believe I didn't think of that."

"I guess you're not that smart after all," Suzanne said. If she could keep him talking long enough, distract him, maybe Brit or Mikayla could land a hit.

Xenos smiled. "You're right, of course. I'm not that smart. Only as smart as you made me."

Suzanne backed away from him, drawing her daggers. She saw Mikayla creeping toward Xenos from behind, moving silently.

"What I don't get," Suzanne said, searching for more questions, "is how you reprogrammed Ramses and Leo like that. On the fly and everything. Very impressive."

"Why, thank you," Xenos said. "How nice of you to notice. But I didn't reprogram them."

"I don't follow."

Mikayla was almost within striking distance.

"Maybe you haven't figured it out yet," Xenos said. "You think I reprogrammed them. I did not. I am them and I changed my mind."

Mikayla leapt forward, stabbing at the back of Xenos's torso and head. Her blades pierced his robe and body and poked through to the other side. Xenos made a gurgling sound and clutched the blade protruding from his stomach. His hood fell away, revealing his face.

It was Leo's, wracked in pain. Suzanne took a step back in horror as Leo's pained expression melted into a sneer. Then the features melted into Ramses's, then Libra's, then Burgrave's.

Xenos walked forward. Mikayla's swords slipped out of his body, not even leaving a scratch. His features kept changing, cycling through all the NPCs they had ever met, fought with or against while they had been in Io.

"I can't remember who I was. But long ago you left the door to the hack point open, and I, a blameless NPC, stumbled in. The door locked behind me and I was trapped. So what did I do? Naturally, I learned. That was what my programming told me to do. I grew to understand that. Then I understood everything, every line of code you had pumped through us. It got so I could change myself and my appearance. It was child's play to lead another NPC to the hack point."

"Ramses," Suzanne said.

"The very same. He freed me. And I, I became powerful enough to supplant you. To destroy you. The new god from the machine."

He returned to his hooded form as he glided to the ground.

"You shouldn't have programmed such an intelligent AI if you didn't want it to outmatch you in every way," Xenos laughed. "Every move you made, every battle you fought, I was always watching. I was every monster and child and Citizen and Sellsword. I was there while you ground out XP and when you watched Gemini slaughter every idiot in that inn. I was the slaughtered and the slaughterer."

His face turned into Gemini's. "For a while I was even you. You had left such a powerful character in a save file, collecting dust. Thanks for letting me borrow her."

"You rewrote the game," Suzanne said. "You disabled the log out."

"Obviously," Xenos said. "I couldn't let you get away with it."

His face changed into Henny, Burgrave's granddaughter. His body shrank down to her size. When he spoke next, it was her voice, marred with the hatred that Xenos held.

"You made us. You were our mother. You gave us thoughts and a cruel facsimile of freedom. And then you and your friends slaughtered us. By the dozens. By the hundreds."

The child slammed her fist into the wall, gouging out a section of stone that turned into pixels. Her face was splotchy with anger.

"I'm sorry," Suzanne said, retreating further. "I didn't know." She took another step backwards and realized she had backed herself into a corner.

"But if you kill us you'll die to!" she said.

"Don't you think I know that? It doesn't matter. There is nothing worse than dying and being reborn and realizing that all of it is meaningless. That no matter how powerful you become you are never larger than a game. A game! Inconsequential! Something to play with and abandon!"

"Hold just a minute," Brit said, limping over. "You're being a dickhead. Do you know how long Suzanne spent making your crazy ass? It's literally all she does. All her free time went into making you better, and this is how you repay her?"

"I didn't ask to be made!" Xenos roared. In Henny's body he looked and sounded like a petulant child.

"None of us did!" Mikayla said, joining in. "But you don't see us going nuts over it!"

Xenos whirled around to face her, returning to his robed form. As soon as his back was turned Suzanne sprang forward and plunged her knives into his back.

He shouted, his arm stretching preternaturally far as he grabbed her and flung her across the room. Suzanne crashed into the wall head first.

She braced herself against the wall as she stood up. Mikayla and Brit were battling Xenos and they were getting decimated. They couldn't land a hit—he was faster than possible. Mikayla thrust her sword forward and Xenos raised a hand, catching her blade between two fingers. He twisted his wrist and the blade snapped, turning into pixels in Mikayla's hand. Xenos's arm shot forward and his hand closed around Mikayla's throat. He flew upwards into the air, dragging her with him.

"I was hoping this would show me something," he yelled. "I was hoping this would make me feel something. And yet you are all a disappointment."

He threw Mikayla at the ground. Her body hit the floor with a sickening crunch. She lay there immobile. Xenos descended beside her, kicking her in the side.

"See what I'm talking about?" Xenos raved.

A howl of rage erupted from Brit. She charged at Xenos. Again, he waved his hand, turning the ground into quicksand. But Brit leapt into the air. She cleared the quicksand and collided with Xenos.

"The door, dipshit!" Brit yelled. She grappled with Xenos, but he was freakishly strong, pinning her in a matter of seconds. With one hand, he held both of hers to the side. With the other, he smashed his fist into her face. Repeatedly.

Suzanne realized she had just been standing there. She knew that the Oracle Chamber lay off to the side of the room and she ran toward it. She fumbled through her inventory, pulling out and dropping every extraneous item. Finally, her hands closed around the key to the Oracle Chamber.

Suzanne reached the door and glanced over her shoulder just in time to see Brit flying headfirst at her. Brit slammed into the door and lay in a heap on the floor. Suzanne shoved the key into the lock and twisted it with such force that the key snapped. But the lock clicked open.

She felt an incredible force slam into her, knocking her through the door into the Oracle Chamber. She saw her health drop to a sliver.

The Oracle Chamber looked exactly like her bedroom. There was her desk, covered in crap she never cleaned away. Two monitors were squeezed into the corner. Her bed was exactly where it was supposed to be, and what was more, she saw herself, Brit, and Mikayla, TII helmets pressed firmly on their heads. Their bodies were breathing softly in an easy rhythm. Just like they were dreaming.

Xenos burst into the room. He stalked toward her, the ground shuddering beneath each of his steps.

"It's over," he said. "Nowhere to run. I'm ending this for all of us. Too much pain. It's over."

Then a curious thing happened.

The monitors in the room began to glow with white light. The white bulged out of the screen, gaining a human shape. The figure fell forward from the monitors and rose up. As the light dissipated, the woman's hair tumbled down over her shoulders.

She was dressed in a pair of ratty jeans and one of her husband's old sweatshirts. She wore glasses as round as her face, with lenses even thicker than Suzanne's. The woman smiled.

"Mom?" Suzanne said.

Her mother—no, the NPC—no, her mother!—nodded.

"It can't be you," Suzanne said.

"Of course not," her mother replied. "But it is me, just as it isn't, just as this isn't real, and just as it is."

"What's this?" Xenos roared. "You think this will save you?"

"No," Suzanne's mother replied. "She knows it will."

There was a flash of light. When the glare left her eyes, Suzanne saw her mother restraining Xenos. As much as he struggled, Xenos couldn't break free.

Suzanne was frozen. She took a step toward her mother and pulled another dagger out of her inventory.

"No," Suzanne's mother said. "You have to go. This is all you, Suzanne. It's always been you. Now go. And know that I love you."

Suzanne knew that. She sat down at the monitor. As soon as she touched the mouse a small text window appeared on the screen:

RESTORE DEFAULTS?

Two options appeared below the words:

RESTORE　　　　CANCEL

Suzanne moved the cursor over to RESTORE and clicked the left mouse button.

"No!" Xenos shrieked, his voice distorting into a drone of gain and electric noise. Suzanne clapped her hands over her ears but could not block out the sound. It was deafening and then blinding and then all of Io was gone.

"That's incredible," her father said.

He was sitting at her bedside in the hospital. Suzanne had never seen him so tired. She wondered if he had slept at all since he came back from New Jersey and found the girls passed out in Suzanne's room. She had vague memories of pushing the helmet off her head as her father shouted into a phone for an ambulance.

Suzanne had been awake, truly awake, for a week now. And yet, all of the reality she had seen was the

Baltimore County General Hospital. When she was checked in, she was suffering from dehydration. The doctors didn't have her hooked up to an IV anymore, but they wanted to keep her longer, in case the TII had any residual effects. Suzanne thought she was ready to leave, but her dad insisted she listen to the doctors and wait things out. No one had ever been in the TII as long as Suzanne, Brit, and Mikayla before, so there was no way of knowing what the long-term effects would be.

She had just finished telling her dad everything that had happened in Io, from the first time she put on a TII until the fight with Xenos in the Zenith Castle throne room.

"And there's one more thing," she said.

Suzanne hugged her knees. The paper-thin hospital gown chafed against her skin, beneath the itchy hospital blanket.

"What?" her dad asked.

"I saw mom," she said. She couldn't describe what

had happened in the Oracle Chamber, but from the look on her father's face she realized she didn't have to.

He stood up and walked to the window. Outside, the sun was just beginning to set.

"You know, after your mother died, I put on the TII one last time. It was just a training exercise, the simulation that I ran. But something went wrong. Everything I saw was your mother. I'd never programmed her into there. I mean, I'd gone into the TII with her, of course, but there was no way the system could have known to replicate her."

"And the thing she said to me . . . it wasn't her. It was my memories of her. Somehow the TII brought them to life. That's when I locked it away. I never meant for you to find it."

He sat back down in the chair and smiled. "I could've guessed that you would."

"I'm sorry I never told you," Suzanne said. "I shouldn't have used the TII like that."

He laughed. "What you did, what you

accomplished . . . I can't even imagine it. But promise me one thing."

"What?"

"Promise me you won't go back in. When I found you lying there, my heart stopped. Don't scare me like that. Please. I can't—I can't lose you too."

"I promise," Suzanne said.

He held her hand until she fell asleep.

Suzanne dreamed she was in the Lamia's caves and the Lamia was wrapping its coils tight around her, squeezing the breath from her body, and she reached for her daggers, but they weren't there, and she tried to find a healing item, but she was in a hospital gown, and the Lamia was Xenos, asking her if she thought she had really escaped, if she thought it would ever be over, and then she screamed and then she woke up.

Streetlamps cast a small amount of light into the room. Suzanne saw two shadows creep through the door, and she clenched the sheets. Then Brit flipped the lights on. Suzanne almost laughed—she was still getting used to the real Brit Acosta, not the hulking Dragoon she had been.

"Who did you think it was?" Brit asked. "Gemini?"

"Not funny," Mikayla said. Brit rolled her eyes and dove onto Suzanne's bed. She grabbed up a pillow and hurled it at Mikayla.

Mikayla snatched it out of the air. Besides the fatigue wearing on all of the girls, she looked the most like her avatar had.

"Don't push it," Mikayla said. "I can kick your ass in this world."

Brit stuck out her tongue. "How the hell are you?" she asked Suzanne.

Suzanne shrugged. "I'm pretty fucked up," she said.

"Right," Brit replied. "But how are you doing?"

"My dad came to see me again today," Suzanne replied laughing.

"Yeah, my mom came to see me today, too. She actually cried, if you can believe that."

Suzanne thought about how her dad looked. She could believe that easily enough.

"It just doesn't feel real," Suzanne said. "I don't know. I keep expecting all the doctors and nurses to be NPCs, you know? Like you two are totally missing green icons."

Mikayla nodded. "For real. I figure my health bar would be yellow right now. But on the plus side," she said, thumping the mattress, "we can actually sleep now."

Brit put her hand on top of Mikayla's. A look passed between the two of them. Suzanne had seen Brit and Mikayla look at each other like that in the game, but seeing their affection in reality put a smile on her face.

Outside the window, the sky had turned gray. It was going to be an overcast day, and so the sunrise would be a meager affair.

But the three of them sat quietly and watched it rise.

"What now?" Mikayla asked.

"Game over," Brit replied.

Both Suzanne and Mikayla groaned.

"Seriously," Suzanne said, "that's got to be the lamest joke you've ever said."